A man's heart plans his way, But the LORD directs his steps.
PROVERBS 16:9

Rosa

A Needful Bride

Danni Roan

Copyright © 2020 Danni Roan

All rights reserved

The characters and events portrayed in this book are fictitious. Any similarity to real persons, living or dead, is coincidental and not intended by the author.

No part of this book may be reproduced, or stored in a retrieval system, or transmitted in any form or by any means, electronic, mechanical, photocopying, recording, or otherwise, without express written permission of the publisher.

ISBN: 9798618465465

Cover design by: Erin Dameron-Hill

Library of Congress Control Number: 2018675309
Printed in the United States of America

Contents

Title Page
Copyright
Epigraph
Introduction
Chapter 1	1
Chapter 2	7
Chapter 3	13
Chapter 4	18
Chapter 5	26
Chapter 6	35
Chapter 7	41
Chapter 8	46
Chapter 9	53
Chapter 10	61
Chapter 11	68
Chapter 12	79

Chapter 13	89
Chapter 14	98
Chapter 15	104
Chapter 16	109
Chapter 17	115
Chapter 18	126
Chapter 19	137
Chapter 20	143
Chapter 21	147
Chapter 22	152
Chapter 23	158
Chapter 24	171
Chapter 25	181
Epilogue	189

Introduction

Rosa Rodriguez is independent for the first time in her life. She has a job she enjoys, and a way to provide for herself and her daughter. Surrounded by friends, she battles the sorrow, anger, and shame of the past, uncertain of what her future could bring. Will her misconceptions, doubts, and lack of trust steal her chance at love?

Dan Gaines has been focused on building his ranch, providing for his men, and caring for the town of Needful. As the reluctant mayor of the tiny cow town, he is determined to meet the needs of all who live there, but one particularly stubborn woman won't let him help. As his frustration turns to infatuation, his feelings of personal guilt over his friend's death keeps him from seeing what is right before his eyes. Will circumstances, misunderstandings, and danger separate him from the one who owns his heart?

Chapter 1

"I don't know what to do," Dan Gaines spun as he made another pass across the floor of his brother's small office, raking his hands through his dark brown hair. "I've tried everything I know, but the guilt is eating me up inside."

"Dan, if she doesn't want to see you there isn't much you can do." Spencer looked at his younger brother; his blue eyes tracking him as he took three paces across the floor then turned again retracing his steps.

"I need to apologize," Dan grumbled, flopping into the single chair in front of Spencer's overcrowded desk. "I didn't mean it."

Spencer Gaines shuffled a few pieces of paper on his desk, flicking through the newest wanted posters that had arrived on the last stage. He'd seen more trouble in the past two weeks from outlaws than he ever expected in the burgeoning cattle town of Needful, Texas. "You could write her a note," Spencer grinned, his blue eyes twinkling with barely suppressed humor.

"And say what?" Dan lifted his head from his hands, meeting his brother's gaze with identical blue eyes. "She'll probably just throw it into the fire unread."

"Little brother, I'm afraid you're going to just have to let this go. Stay out of her way, and it will blow over soon, I'm sure."

Dan sprang to his feet again, cutting his brother a hard glare. "What if she needs something? What if Christina gets sick again? What if some other outlaws decide to kidnap her?"

"Then we'll deal with it?" Spencer said a hard edge in his voice. Two weeks ago he wouldn't have expected to be so calm about the situation, but he, his brother and several other of the town's men had rescued Rosa Rodriguez and Ruth Rivers from a band of outlaws, bringing them both home safely and sending the outlaws to jail at the same time. "Besides, she has the Hamptons."

"But she doesn't have to work. I told her I'd get her a place, give her and Christina a home. Pay for everything. It's my fault she lost Raul. If I hadn't kept sending him to Mexico to buy cattle or bring back horses, this never would have happened. They could have the little spread they wanted and be raising their daughter together."

Spencer pushed himself out of his chair and stepped around the desk. "Dan, I know you're speaking from the heart," he mused lightly as he clapped a hand on his brother's shoulder. "I know you feel responsible for what happened to Raul and how he died, but it isn't your fault."

Dan twisted out of his brother's grasp as guilt gnawed at his middle. "You can say that, but I know better. Rosa shouldn't have to work day in and day out at the Hampton House to support herself and Christina. If only she would listen to reason."

Spencer handed his brother his hat from the rack by the door. "Come on over for lunch with me and Daliah," he offered opening the door. "You're gonna make yourself sick worryin' on this. You need to let it go."

Dan huffed out a sigh, slapping his hat on his head as they stepped out of the tiny sheriff's office and jail. "No, I'm headed home," he growled. "I'm better off when I'm working, anyway. I'll see you Sunday."

Spencer shrugged, pulling the door closed behind him. "Suit yourself," he mumbled, knowing that nothing he said would change his brother's mind. Raul Rodriguez had been killed by bounty hunters well over a year ago. The big man, a hard worker, and a dedicated family man had been mistaken for his outlaw brother and shot down in cold blood. For whatever reason, Dan had decided it was his fault that Raul was dead and that as mayor Dan needed to see to the man's family.

Since Rosa had been kidnapped, his worry, frustration, and determination had flared to a fevered pitch.

"Go home, Dan," Spencer said. "Leave Rosa alone. If she needs something we're all here for her."

Dan dragged his pony's reins from the hitching post on the main drag through town and stepped down into the dusty street. A cool breeze whipped in from the prairie, swirling little puffs of dust around his boots as he tossed himself up into the saddle and turned north toward home. "Give Daliah and Chad my love," he said sagging in the saddle as his horse stepped into a trot.

"Was that Dan?" A woman's voice drifted down the boardwalk, and Spencer turned, a bright smile gracing his handsome face.

"That was Dan," Spencer offered. "I invited him to join us for lunch, but he wouldn't stay."

Daliah wrapped her fingers into her husband's hand and smiled. "You need to give him time," she said her dark eyes scanning his face as she brushed a stray dark-gold curl from her face. "He has a lot on his mind right now."

Spencer nodded, following his wife around the corner of the jailhouse toward their small home. "I don't like him being so obsessed with Rosa and her plight," the lawman shook his head but looked up when Daliah squeezed his hand. "It's not like him."

"Dan feels responsible," Daliah spoke, her voice soft. Everything about her was soft, warm, and loving, and it made Spencer's once cold heart glow with warmth. "He's the Mayor of Needful, and Raul worked for him as much as he did anyone else. He feels like he needs to fix things."

"Honey, I don't think this can be fixed. Rosa is still angry with Raul for getting himself killed. If he hadn't taken that loan from his outlaw brother, he never would have been in that border town where he was killed."

"Maybe now that you've put that same outlaw brother in jail, she'll be able to forgive her late husband," Daliah's soft smile ushered them through the door of the light blue house. "It takes time to get over a shock like that, and the grief that goes with it."

Spencer released her hand to dip his fingers into the basin of clean water by the door, washing some of the worry from his face with a splash. Daliah had known enough grief in her own life, but she still found love and understanding for others. Drying his face, he followed her into the house and breathed in the smell of fresh bread and boiled eggs.

"No one has it easy all the time," Daliah said smoothing her apron. "Every person has to work through their grief and anger in their own way, and nothing Dan does can fix that for Rosa. He needs to give her space."

Spencer leaned over, placing his hands on Daliah's hips and stealing a kiss. "How d'you ever get to be so wise?" he asked, a teasing light flickering in his eyes.

"I watch," she grinned, kissing him back.

"You're too good for me, you know that right?"

Daliah's soft laugh filled the small house as she snagged his hand once more and pulled him toward the table. "Let's eat," she chortled. "I have to go see Peri after lunch. She said Prim isn't feeling well."

"Nothing serious I hope." Spencer looked up from where he had slipped into a chair.

"Nothing seven or eight months won't cure," Daliah laughed.

Chapter 2

Olive Hampton shook her head as the stream of sharp Spanish words floated from the kitchen.

Ever since her chief cook and friend Rosa Rodriguez had been kidnapped by her erstwhile brother-in-law, the woman had been a simmering pot about to boil over. No one dared invade the kitchen other than to slip the prepared meals out the door quietly, and no matter how often Olive had tried, Rosa refused to talk about the events.

More rapid-fire Spanish peppered the air and Olive cringed. She didn't understand the language well but had the impression that the tiny Mexican woman was calling down fire and brimstone on someone's head.

"It's terrible quiet in the place," Orville said stepping up to his wife and slicking his white hair back with one hand. "The men of the town are half afraid to eat here what with all that," he nodded toward the kitchen door before his dark eyes turned back to his wife. "We didn't start this boarding house and eatery to be run out of business. I hope she gets this out of her system soon."

Olive placed her hand on Orville's arm, squeezing gently. "You'd think that now that Spencer sent Rivera and his gang off to prison, she'd simmer down," the older woman said, "but something seems to keep her on a low boil all the time. I offered to take Christina for a spell, but she won't let her baby girl out of her site for five minutes."

"Did Ruth say anything? She was there with Rosa through the whole mess and seems to be alright."

Orville shook his head, cringing as something clattered loudly in the kitchen. "I'll talk to Darwin out at the livery," he cringed again at the sound of a pan scraping across the hot cook stove. "Darwin seems to have come to accept that his wife can look after herself since this misadventure at least, and they're happy." The old man grinned, his eyes sparkling with delight at the young couple who had gone through so much to find true love.

"In other words, you're escaping to the barn," Olive placed her hands on her hips and shot her husband an accusatory glance.

"You bet!" Orville chuckled, leaning in and kissing her cheek. "Let me know when it's safe to come home," he added with a laugh. "And don't forget about the buttermilk," he paused, turning to meet Olive's soft gaze. "Rosa's cookin' is as hot as her temper recently, and we'll need it to wash down every bite."

Olive's soft laughter trailed the old man out of the Hampton House dining room, and he couldn't help but sigh in relief when the warm air brushed away his nerves.

***

"Mayor Dan," Orville called waving as a lean cowboy slipped off his horse, tying it to the hitching post with a quick flick of the reins. "Haven't seen you about much this week."

"I've been busy," Dan growled, his blue eyes flashing at Orville and the old man scowled. He'd kept to the ranch for more than a week after his conversation with his brother, but couldn't take it anymore.

"You looking for a meal?"

Dan nodded, some of his irritation ebbing.

"Well be prepared, Rosa's cooking everything extra hot. If you can stomach it, there's plenty to be had."

Dan quirked a dark brow, looking at Orville questioningly. "She's alright isn't she?"

"Seems fine other than her temper stewing like a pot of spicy soup. Ever since you and the other men rescued her and Ruth, she's been in a foul mood. Stormin' round the kitchen talkin' too herself and banging the pots and pans like drums. I'd think she would be relieved to be back safe and sound with little Christina."

Dan nodded slowly, his eyes turning toward the Hampton House front door, and a slow burn crept up his cheeks. "I'm sure she'll settle down in time." His blue eyes flicked between Orville and the door. "It was a very stressful time, and everyone is still processing what happened."

"Is there something we should know about?" Orville eyed the younger man suspiciously. "I mean Ruth told us what happened and all, but she seems fine while Rosa's angry as a wet hen in the ice house."

Dan pulled his hat from his head and ran a hand through his thick locks before crushing the brim of the already battered hat in his hand. "Not that I know of," he mumbled turning and stepping up on the boardwalk.

Orville squinted at the Mayor of Needful, Texas sure he was missing something. The man's spine was ramrod straight, his hands clenched around his hat, and an expression of hard determination covered his handsome face. There was more to the tale of Rosa and Ruth's abduction than Mayor Dan was telling, and sooner or later, Orville would figure it out. In the meantime, he hoped his stomach could deal with the flaming meals his full-time cook and usually sweet friend was dishing out.

"Lord, somethin's going on that I haven't twigged to yet," the old man said looking up at a cloudless late-summer sky. "You'll help us out with it when you're ready though, so I'll just get on about my business until you do."

Spinning on his heel, Orville strode toward the large livery stable where the sound of cheery whistling was drifting into the air. At least one person in Needful was happy.

***

Dan stepped into the boarding house and stopped, looking around at the few patrons seated at tables scattered through the long room. Usually at this time of day the restaurant was packed with farmers, miners, and cowboys looking for a hot meal and a break from the labors of the day.

Several of his own hands nodded in his direction then turned their eyes back to stare at the bowls of stew before them.

"What's wrong?" Dan finally asked, stepping up to a few punchers he had sent to town for supplies.

"You'd need a cast-iron belly to eat this chow," the man grumbled. "Rosa seems to have opened every chili powder she owns into the pot today."

Dan bent low, leaning over the bowl and taking a sniff, pulling back sharply as his eyes burned.

"I'm bringin' more bread," Olive Hampton bustled into the room, a heavy tray in her hands. "It helps with the spices and Shi is bringing buttermilk." She smiled around her, but her eyes were troubled.

"Why are you baking in the living quarters?" Dan asked, his eyes flicking toward the kitchen door where he could just hear Rosa's voice.

"We're lettin' Rosa have her space." Olive cut her eyes to the cattle rancher and mayor of her new home. "She's still a little upset after her unfortunate adventure."

Dan nodded and Olive scowled. Was that a flash of guilt across the man's face?

"You have a seat, and I'll get you a meal," Olive offered, gesturing around the mostly empty room.

"Do you think I could speak to Rosa?" Dan looked up, his blue eyes worried. "I'd like to discuss what happened."

Olive watched the man's Adam's apple bob and gasped. "I don't think that's a good idea," she said. "Rosa's riled up about something, and until her temper ebbs, it's best to give her some room."

"I'm sorry Olive but I need to speak to her." Dan squared his shoulders and looked toward the kitchen as he stepped around the older woman.

Chapter 3

Dan Gaines filled his lungs with air and stepped forward, his face set as if walking to the gallows. He hadn't meant to upset Rosa when he and the town posse had swept into the outlaw Rivera's camp to rescue the women that had been abducted.

"Rosa," he whispered as he reached the doorway, his eye taking in the slim woman slamming pans around on the hot stove. She was stunning. Her black hair tied into a tight braid that fell below her knees, her slim form wrapped in a deep red dress with wide ruffled skirts.

In one corner of the kitchen, a little girl sat behind an odd fence playing with a doll, but she pushed herself to her feet, a bright toothy smile spreading across her face as she saw him. Dan's heart warmed gazing at tiny Christina who latched her pudgy hands on the top rail of the fence and bounced with a giggle.

"You!" Rosa twirled toward Dan, brandishing a ladle like a weapon. "Why are you here," her dark eyes squinted and she glared at him in anger.

"I wanted to speak to you," Dan replied, stepping into the room. "To apologize."

"No, you go!" Rosa spat. "I do not want to see you. I do not want to know that you exist. Go now."

"Rosa," Dan splayed his hands before him, imploring her to listen. "We need to talk about what happened. Let me explain."

Rosa took a step closer, placing one hand on her hip and waving the ladle in Dan's face. "I do not want to know. You have no right to bother me. I am a good woman. Honest. Faithful. True. You go. I do not want to see your face."

Dan huffed out a breath, his anger rising. "Why can't you listen to me?" he barked. "I'm here to explain if you'll give me a minute."

"No!" Rosa whirled back to the stove, plunging the ladle into a large stew pot with a harsh clatter.

"Rosa,"

"Don't you Rosa me," the petite woman snarled, whipping back in a flutter of skirts and shaking her finger at him. "You have no right to bother me. You are not my husband and not my friend. Go. Away."

"No." Dan's stomach quivered as he met Rosa's dark eyes. She needed to understand about the mistake that he could never regret.

The stream of Spanish that hit him as Rosa threw her hands in the air was like a wave crashing over him and threatening to pull him under, and Dan staggered back as the woman approached.

"Rosa," he tried again but was drowned out by her rapid-fire words. He had no idea what she was saying, but the sharp poke of her finger in his chest was painful as she backed him into the opposite wall.

"Rosa," he tried again, but she only snarled and spun to return to her stove.

"Go!" she bellowed, stirring the heavy pot.

Dan took a step forward, determined to get through to the stubborn woman. He had made a mistake, but he only wanted to be sure she was cared for. He had offered her a little house on his property several times over the past year and a half, but she wouldn't accept it, instead insisting on living out her days in this stuffy kitchen with no hope for a better tomorrow.

"Rosa," his voice was soft, imploring. "Please listen."

Rosa Rodriguez grasped the handle of the stew pot, her eyes prickling with unshed tears as her anger at the man burned hotter than the spices in the stew.

"I didn't mean," Dan stuttered, stepping one pace closer. "I mean..."

The pot shot from the stove in a swift gesture, hurtling toward him and dumping its contents like hot oil from the parapet of a castle.

Dan Gaines's eyes grew wide as he dove for the door, tucking as his hands hit the hard plank floor and rolling in a quick somersault that placed him back on his feet. Grabbing his hat he raced for the front door in a racket of harsh words, loud laughter, and the sound of pounding hoofbeats.

***

Olive gaped as the town's mayor raced out her door and charged away on the cow pony that must have been waiting outside. She had warned him not to try to talk to Rosa in her current state, but he hadn't listened and now look at the mess they were in.

Turning slowly, she pinned the laughing cowhands with her dark eyes. "Something is happening here," she spoke, her lips pinching as she glared. "Do any of you know what's going on between Rosa and Mayor Dan?"

The roll of laughter snapped like a taut string breaking to silence and the men shot nervous glances at each other then looked back to Olive shaking their heads.

Something more than Rosa being frightened by her former brother-in-law was going on. Olive was sure of it, and someone must know what it was.

One way or another she would get to the bottom of this. Whatever it took.

"Mother Olive," a sweet voice made Olive turn, her shoulders sagging as her quietest daughter-in-law Ellen looked at her.

"What is it dear?" Olive sighed as a dull throb started between her eyes.

"Arabela sent Rosa away," Ellen said softly, twisting her apron in her hands, her blonde head dipped low. "I'll clean up the mess."

"Mess?" Olive asked. "What mess?"

Ellen took her mother-in-law by the hand and pulled her toward the kitchen and the pot of stew oozing across the floor. "Oh my!"

"Don't worry," a black-haired beauty standing next to the hot stove like a queen about to hold court, said turning to smile at Olive. "Rosa will be back, but I sent her out for a while. Shi is taking Christina for a walk, and Ellen said she'd clean up while I start on supper. Honestly mother Hampton," she continued. "I'll be glad to eat something that doesn't burn your insides out."

A nervous laugh filled the kitchen as all three women grinned, letting the tension of the week slip from their shoulders. At least life wasn't dull in Needful.

Chapter 4

Rosa paced across the clearing at the back of the Hampton House, her heavy skirts dragging through the dust unheeded.

No one had ever been able to make her as angry as the Mayor of Needful. Well, perhaps once upon a time her father. She spat in the dust, spinning again as a breeze teased at the hair that had been freed from her long braid.

Pausing, the petite Mexican woman sucked in a breath of air, letting it out slowly as the tears she held in check threatened to fall.

She had wanted to rant at Arabela. To scold and shout, but the woman's haughty blue eyes and raised brow had stopped Rosa from giving in to her instincts. She had been acting like a rabid dog, but every time she thought back to the rescue, her temper flared once more.

Rosa Rodriguez had been through enough in her short life. She had thought that marrying Raul was the answer to all of her troubles, but with him gone she was on her own, and it frightened her. Still, she would rather live her life in service to the Hamptons than agree to Dan Gaines and his proposal. She would not make the mistakes of her mother. She had a roof over her head, a place for her sweet baby girl, and friends. Perhaps she had started as the hired help here at the boarding house, but now she knew the Hamptons were almost family.

Guilt squirmed in her middle at how she had been treating her friends, but the anger that burned in her had blazed so brightly that she hadn't given a thought to her behavior. Those who loved her shouldn't have to suffer for the sins of one man. A hint of a smile touched her lips as she thought of throwing the pot of stew at the town's mayor then she cringed at what it would cost Olive and Orville to replace the wasted food.

No, she had to get herself under control. Calm down and make her life better. Losing Raul, a man she had loved dearly, had been devastating, but she couldn't give up. She had a daughter to care for. Friends who loved her and a new home to build. Daniel Gaines, mister almighty cattle rancher, and mayor could go soak his head for all she cared.

Rosa brushed her fingers over her lips as her rebellious body remembered the press of Dan's lips on hers and heat stirred unbidden. He was a handsome man but had no honor. No, she would stay away from the Mayor of Needful and hold tight to her pride. She would not repeat the sins of the past. Her daughter would have a life with joy, peace, and respect. Rosa had left Mexico and the pain of the past behind when Raul had started a farm in Texas. She would continue in her new life unfettered by sin.

***

"Rosa, Rosa?" Ruth Rivers' voice filtered into Rosa's weary brain and she turned toward the small house at the other end of the yard where the plump young woman waved cheerfully. "Come have tea with me?"

Rosa sighed but nodded, lifting her skirts and giving them a shake to rid them of most of the dust her nervous pacing had caused.

"Are you finally taking some time off?" Ruth asked, her eyes glinting behind round spectacles. "I told you, you needed time to rest after what happened." Ruth grabbed Rosa's arm, pulling her toward the front door of the small single room house. "Wait till you see what Darwin bought me," the other woman gushed.

Rosa grinned at Ruth's infectious cheerfulness. She had grown close to the newest Needful Bride as she had taught her to cook and clean over the summer.

"What has your man done for you now?" she asked as they stepped into the darker recesses of the house. The afternoon breeze ruffled bright yellow curtains at the open windows and Rosa looked around the simple home trying to spot anything new.

The small trunk Ruth had brought with her still sat in front of the stone fireplace skirted by two chairs, the large bentwood bed looked comfortable and inviting with a new quilt spread across it and two more trunks stood at attention on the far side of the room. Rosa couldn't see what Ruth was so excited about.

"There," Ruth gushed still holding Rosa's arm and pointing into the fireplace where a miniature stove stood, sparkling with shiny chrome and pristine white porcelain.

"You have a real stove!" Rosa gushed, turning to hug her friend. "Your Darwin, he is a good man."

"He is," Ruth blushed "and there's so much more happening, but that's for another time." She winked cheekily and moved the kettle onto the burner. "We're having a tea party."

Rosa laughed and more of the anger and tension she had been holding so tightly to sloughed away like shards of broken shale.

Rosa took a seat by the small trunk that served as a table for two and watched Ruth prepare the tea. When the other woman had arrived in Needful, she hadn't even known how to boil water, but she was becoming a proficient cook and homemaker. Rosa squirmed in her seat, remembering how she had been storming in the kitchen since her safe return, virtually banishing everyone from her domain. Surely Ruth had missed their days working at the big oven, and Rosa's face heated with shame at her selfishness.

By the time she was six-years-old, Rosa had been cooking, cleaning, and caring for her mother's richly appointed home and tending her younger siblings. It seemed that every second year there was a new child added, and each one made Rosa sag more heavily with shame.

She had gone to the priests in her tiny town lighting candles and praying that her mother's shame would end, but it never did. The priest had offered little hope, but each time she looked at the polished crucifix at the front of the cathedral she pleaded once more for a chance to escape the lifestyle of her family. Jesus had looked down on her in silent sorrow and love, but still, nothing changed.

"You look troubled," Ruth's voice was soft; kind. "Are you still upset about what happened? You're safe now and everyone here is looking out for you." Ruth reached across the trunk, patting Rosa's hand, relieved when her friend finally lifted her dark eyes and met hers.

"It is, how you say, complicated." Rosa shook her head. She couldn't speak to even Ruth about her past. She couldn't bear the look of horror and disgust that would surely fall on her once the sweet woman knew.

"Rosa you are not alone anymore," Ruth said removing her hand and grasping the simple brown teapot as she poured the bubbling brew. "You know you can tell me anything. I love you."

Rosa smiled sadly, wondering what the other woman would feel if only she knew. Rosa had escaped the life of shame, leaving her family behind when Raul had fallen in love with her. Her mother had been livid when she had run away at the tender age of seventeen with the paunchy caballero with the quick smile and sparkling eyes, but she had escaped and would never go back.

"It has been a very hard time," Rosa said taking the cup Ruth handed her. "In time things will go back to normal, and all will be well."

"Has Dan been to see you again?" Ruth asked, a twinkle entering her eye.

Rosa raised her chin, her dark eyes flashing with anger. "I do not want to see that man," she spat. "I will poison him the next time he tries to speak to me."

Ruth blinked, leaning away from the other woman's wrath. Surely a kiss, in the heat of the moment, hadn't been enough to inspire such anger in her friend.

"Rosa, you need to forgive him." Ruth shook her head, lifting her cup and saucer with care. "He didn't mean any disrespect. He was just relieved to find us safe. We could have both been murdered or worse!"

Rosa's face grew cold. "I do not need to forgive him. He had no right to do what he did." Rosa waved a hand as if brushing a speck of dust from her dress. "He is not a good man."

Ruth bit her lip, not knowing what to say. She loved Rosa, but she couldn't agree with her on this. Ruth didn't know Mayor Dan well, but he had a reputation as a well-liked and honorable man. "How can you say that?" Ruth met Rosa's eyes over her teacup. "Everyone speaks highly of him. His men respect him, and if he were a scoundrel, I'm sure he never would have been elected Mayor."

Rosa snorted, a very unladylike sound in contrast to the lovely china cup she held in her hands. "There are many men who have a good reputation in their community, but hide their dirty secrets in the dust of the country."

Ruth could see that there was no point arguing with her friend, so she let the subject drop but filed away the comment for further investigation at a later date. "How is Christina?" Ruth asked, changing the subject and sighing when Rosa smiled.

"Ellen took her for a walk," Rosa said. "She has been too much inside with me these past few days. I have been selfish."

"Rosa, you have been through a traumatic experience," Ruth *tsked*. "Don't be so hard on yourself. If I had a child, I wouldn't let her out of my sight after that." Ruth blushed, gazing into her teacup so that Rosa wouldn't see the twinkle in her eye. She had a secret, and as soon as she found the right words to tell Darwin, she would let everyone else know as well.

Chapter 5

Dan was in a foul mood as he rode into the ranch yard and gazed about him. His big barn and neat outbuildings usually cheered him on a hard day, but today no surge of joy greeted him as he stepped down and tossed his reins to a wrangler.

"Boss," the man greeted, but the tall cowboy stalked toward his house without hearing. If he had been a drinking man, he may have wasted his time and money in the town's single saloon, but instead, he had ridden home, the heat of embarrassment and frustration riding his back.

"What's eatin' him?" the wrangler asked as another hand joined him at the corral.

"Only two things get a man riled like that," the older man grinned. "A woman or money trouble."

"We ain't gonna miss our pay are we?" the younger cowhand asked. "I'm savin' up to put in an order for one of them brides Olive and Peri order up for Needful. I almost got enough to put a bit down on a patch of dirt and pay for train fare."

The older man thumped his friend on the

shoulder and laughed. "Dan Gaines is a careful man," he intoned. "I don't reckon, unless we have a bad drought or the like, we'll miss a payday."

"Then why would he be havin' woman trouble?" The younger hand scratched under his hat then stripped the saddle from his boss's horse turning it into the corral. "He didn't order no bride."

***

Dan stormed into his little house. The simple four bedroom building was bigger than he needed, but he'd tried to plan for the future and had made room for his brother Spencer and his son Chad. Dan had sent for them once he had the ranch up and running and had hoped his brother would partner with him at the ranch, but things had gone in a different direction for both of them.

Striding into the large kitchen, Dan gazed around him and groaned when he didn't see his cook at the stove. The man was out at the round-up feeding the crew, and Dan had forgotten to order a meal at the Hampton House as well.

Tossing his hat on the table, he slumped into a chair and pressed his face into his hands. It had been a long day, and it wasn't even suppertime yet. He couldn't understand what Rosa's problem was. Sure, he'd made a few mistakes with the woman, but that couldn't be helped, and he only wanted to help her.

How many times had he offered to set her up with a place of her own? Somewhere she could raise Christina in peace. He was willing to pay for all of it. If only she would agree.

Pushing himself to his feet, he took a turn around the scrubbed table looking at his home. It was simple but well set up with a modern kitchen and sturdy furniture that served him and his crew well.

He wouldn't consider himself a wealthy man, but Dan Gaines had done well for himself and his men. Leaving behind his former home and the ravages of the War Between the States, he had struck out for new territory to find his destiny. What he had found was wild cattle in the hill country of Texas and a collection of men, battered and bloodied by the war, who were willing to risk life and limb to build something from nothing.

Raking his hands through his hair, Dan thought back to those hard years in harsh surroundings where he and a handful of men who had followed his command drew a line in the dusty earth of Texas and marked it as their own.

***

Texas, July 1865

"Where you headed Cap'n?" Jake Anson asked as he pushed his weary mount up next to the man he had followed for the past three years.

"I don't know, Jake." Dan turned in the saddle, studying the six men dogging his heels. When they had been mustered out of the Northern Army a few months earlier most of his soldiers had drifted home, but these men had stayed with him. Most of them had nothing to go back to and were looking for a place to put the past behind them.

"Water up ahead," A lean rider called galloping toward him, his horse panting in the heavy heat of a summer day.

"We'll make camp ahead," Dan said waving the others forward. Most of them still wore their blue and gold uniform trousers but had shed the heavy coats days ago as they'd been hit by waves of heat in this new land. Now, in nothing but shirt sleeves or suspenders and union suits, they sweltered in the afternoon sun.

The small column ambled toward the small river as their horses lifted into an eager trot. The sun was headed toward the horizon and Dan wondered if the night would be cool again. Behind the last rider, a string of war horses laden with heavy packs picked up their pace. Everything the men could beg, or barter for was wrapped in those packs and the future of each of them weighed heavily on Dan's shoulders.

As the march through the southern states had sapped his hope and joy, it had also provided hints and rumors of a new life to Daniel Gaines and his men. He'd heard rumors of wildland still available in the heart of Texas, and the stories of wild cows just waiting to be rounded up pulled him deep into the state.

With a deep history of independence, fighting spirit, and wide-open spaces, Texas beckoned, and Dan had answered the call. He hadn't planned on others wanting to join him, but when several of his men had saddled up and turned west with him, he hadn't argued. It would be good to have men he could trust at his back as they stepped into a new life.

The river came into view and the men let their horses have their heads as they rushed to the water that sparkled with golden light. A light breeze stirred the water, and a dark snake undulated across the cool water.

Mindful of the viper, Dan swung down and moved away from the horses to fill his canteen in the surprisingly cold water.

"Looks like it's spring-fed," Dozer Yokes called filling his canteen. "I reckon the springs upstream a bit based on the flow." The older man grinned, his sleepy-looking eyes that had garnered his name, blinking lazily.

"You willing to scout it?" Dan asked.

"Give the word Cap'n."

Dan groaned. "I'm not your captain anymore,"

he grumbled. "It's ridiculous for a man your age to be deferring to me."

The other man chuckled, peeking out from under heavy lids. "Far as I'm concerned you're still in charge," he grinned.

"See if you can find the spring." Dan shook his head. One way or another, he would get his men to stop looking to him to lead. They were all free men and could do whatever they wanted. At the moment they seemed inclined to go along with this mad dream of his, so he'd just have to deal with it.

Sunlight sparkled off the water, and Dan motioned for the men to let the horses graze while they waited for Dozer to report. It would be good to stop for a while, and though they hadn't been pushing hard as they had so often done in the past, he was hoping their long march was almost over.

The sound of cattle bawling somewhere on the other side of the river made everyone look up as they eased saddle cinches and slipped bridles from their horses.

"You think them's the wild ones?" a younger man called trying to look across the water.

"Reckon we'll know soon enough," another man called out.

"I've never chased cows," the younger man said. "Are they dangerous?" he swallowed, trying to catch a glimpse of the animals they could now hear.

As the men settled in the dust of the prairie, holding loosely to their horses' leads, they watched as first one and then more of the long-horned cattle approach. Even across the small river, they could see the depth and breadth of the beasts. The lead cow stood a good sixteen hands at the shoulder, and the long pointed horns that spanned a good six feet from tip to tip glinted like steel.

"That's what we're here for?" the younger man, Teddy, said swallowing hard as the lead cow huffed as it approached the water.

"That's them," Dan nodded. "We'll have to be smart and work hard, but this is a chance at a new beginning." He lifted his eyes, watching as the cattle shuffled down the banks of the small river and began to drink, keeping a wary eye on the men on the other shore.

"They look dangerous," Teddy whispered.

"They are dangerous," another soldier drawled. "They'll kill ya soon as look at ya, but they got sense too. Cows ain't especially smart, but they have a sense of self-preservation. You point 'em in the direction you want and hold 'em together, they'll move."

"Greg, stop scaring the boy," Dozer rode up watching the cattle gathering on the far shore. "I found the spring," he reported. "About a mile upstream there's a big pool fair grazing and no sign of nobody else."

"Mount up boys," Dan called noting the way the cows swung as one away from the water and back toward the prairie before stopping and watching the men mount up and ride out. "We might have just found a home."

As a group, the men topped out on a low hill that rolled away from the river and sprawled out into grasslands. A shimmering pool glistened gold and orange in the fading rays of the sun. Turning in his saddle, Dan gazed back along their trail catching glimpses of the large herd spreading out along the waterway. It was good land, good grazing, and plenty of water. Pulling a map from his saddlebags he studied the terrain noting the nearest towns and undesignated wild areas.

"Doesn't look like anyone has staked a claim," he said lifting his eyes once more. "We'll make camp and explore more tomorrow. If this is the river I see on the map, it flows into a larger one about forty miles south and leads further toward the gulf from there."

"What do we do now?" Teddy asked, his thin face serious as his dark eyes, far too serious and haunted, scanned the open land.

"Make camp!" Dan yelled.

***

Dan pushed himself up from his solid kitchen chair and grabbed his hat. If dinner wasn't coming to him, he would go to dinner.

"Dozer!" He shouted, striding out the door and across the yard. "Get me a horse."

Chapter 6

The sun was low on the horizon by the time Dan reached the cow camp in the wide rolling plains of his ranch land.

Cattle grazed across the late summer grass and calves frolicked near their watchful mothers.

A sense of peace washed over the Mayor of Needful as he trotted to the battered chuck wagon and called to the cook. The old man with the wispy beard barked an insult at him making him laugh as he stepped from the saddle and swaggered to the fire.

Grabbing a heavy leather pad, Dan reached for the coffee pot pouring the acidic black brew into a mug and taking a swig. "I see your coffee is just as foul as always Cookie," he laughed letting the hot beverage cool slightly in the soft breeze.

"What you doin' out here?" the old man asked, his Rheumy eyes studying Dan suspiciously. "I figured you'd be in town eatin' at that fancy boarding house."

Dan shook his head sipping his coffee then

shaking his head. "Things there are too hot for me Cookie," he drawled. "I figured I'd be safer with your bland, tasteless stew." Dan's blue eyes twinkled as the skinny cook turned, shaking a wooden spoon in his face.

"Tasteless!" the old man bellowed working his bearded jaw. "Why you no good scaly-wag," he continued stomping his feet in the sand and glaring at his boss. "You're lucky I don't poison you for that insult."

Dan's eyes twinkled with delight as the old man groused and stormed, banging pots and pans into the boxes of his wagon. Cookie never really changed. His old blue pants were tucked into battered boots that looked too big for his thin frame. Bright yellow suspenders stood out in contrast to his navy blue wool shirt.

"You know I'm just teasing," Dan laughed as the old man settled, casting him one last glare. "I'm afraid I'm not having any luck with cooks today." Dan shook his dark head hoping Cookie wouldn't throw a pot at him the way Rosa had.

"That bad, huh?" the old man asked walking over to peer into Dan's face. "You look like somethin's troublin' you fierce like."

Dan nodded staring into his cup at the dark depths of coffee. The brown-black brew shimmered in the setting sun making him think of the light in Rosa's dark eyes.

The old cook moved to the heavy iron pot sitting over the fire and gave it a stir then twisted a large skillet of biscuits sitting on a rack slung below the pot. "Must be a woman," the old man whispered then cackled as Dan's head snapped up. "That's what I thought. Why don't you tell me what's goin' on, and maybe my years of worldly experience can he'p you figure out what to do next."

Dan raised a dark brow at the old cook. He'd hired the man to cook for the crew shortly after they had set to gathering a herd on this very patch of land. The old man had wondered into camp half-starved and staggering from a wound to his leg. He'd asked for food but promised to pay in the only way he knew how, telling a hair-raising tale of his escape from desperadoes to the south. Since that day the man everyone called Cookie had cooked and entertained them with tall tales from places far and wide.

"Cookie, I don't know if you have a story that can help with this problem. I just want to make up for my own mistakes and fix a problem. The woman is incidental to the whole issue."

The loud harrumph from the old man made Dan scowl, staring with his mouth half-open.

"No woman is ever incidental, to no tale" the old man growled. "Women make a mess of everythin'," he continued. "You mark my words; things will get worse before they get better. Now spill or you'll be eatin' burnt beef and blackened beans."

Dan chuckled but tried to explain how he wanted to help Rosa and Christine since he hadn't been able to help Raul. He felt responsible for the family who had lost their guardian and provider. It felt good to pour it all out to someone. Spencer had been no help at all. With his worries about the town's safety and a family of his own, half the time Dan was pretty sure his older brother had been secretly laughing at him behind his back. At least the men who had ridden in the posse had agreed to keep quiet about his stupid mistake when they had discovered Ruth and Rosa safe.

Old Cookie slapped his knee as Dan finished his story. "Son, you got more trouble than you even know," he cackled. "Why you got so much trouble, you don't even know what trouble you got."

Dan stood to his feet anger burning through him as he tossed his coffee into the dirt and glared. "What's the point of telling you if all you're going to do is make fun of me?" He snarled leaning over and hissing when the old man grabbed his knees falling back onto the ground in peals of laughter. "I didn't come here to have you poke fun at me."

"Calm down," the old man laughed trying to get himself back under control as he climbed back to his feet dusting his britches. "I ain't gonna tell no one about this. 'sides sounds like enough already know even if they ain't talkin'." Again, a chuckle rolled through him, and he wiped his eyes as tears of mirth raced down his dusty cheeks. "You young folks is always in a hurry. Impatient and such. Some things take time Dan. There are things in this life that can't be rushed." Cookie laid his hand on the younger man's shoulder as Dan sank back on the stool by the fire while other riders approached.

"I hope you have some idea what to do," he finally whispered. "I'm at my wit's end."

The old man's chuckle did nothing to quell the nerves jumping in Dan's stomach, but it was too late now. He'd poured out everything to the old fellow who had earned every man's trust over the years. He only hoped it was worth it. One way or another, he was determined to help the young widow. If he had been a better friend to her husband, she wouldn't be in this situation.

"I just want to help," Dan whispered, hanging his head. "Raul was my friend." The lean rancher squirmed uncomfortably on his seat as the old man studied his face.

"I understand," Cookie chuckled. "Maybe more than you do."

"What's that supposed to mean?" Dan sprang to his feet once more, his blue eyes glinting. "What are you trying to say, old man?"

"Simmer down," the cook said. "I ain't sayin'

nothin'. You young folks sure are skittish nowadays." Cookie chuckled his eyes twinkling as he watched his boss fidget. "One thing I will tell ya though is plain as the nose on your face. If you ain't willin' to do this God's way, you and Rosa and even little Christina may be in for a world of hurt."

Dan scuffed the toe of his boot in the sand but avoided the old man's eyes as something cold crept up his spine. He knew he was partly responsible for what had happened to his onetime wrangler and friend. Taking care of Raul's wife and daughter was the least he could do.

A vision of Rosa's warm brown eyes swam before him, and Dan shoved it away. He couldn't deny that she was a beautiful woman, but she was his friend's wife. "I'm willing to pay whatever it takes to see she's cared for," he whispered.

Chapter 7

Dawn broke and Rosa hurried to the kitchen tying an apron around her slim waist. She was tired and still angry about what had happened to her and Ruth only a few short weeks ago. At least that is what she kept telling herself, but the truth was she had been less frightened in Rivera's clutches than she was of the feelings in her own heart.

"Ellen!" Rosa gasped as she stepped into the already warm cooking area of the Hampton House. "What are you doing?"

"I'm cooking," the pretty blonde wife of Joe Hampton, grinned. "Olive thinks you need a couple of days off."

"But I am the one who cooks." Rosa stared at Ellen in shock. "Miss Olive hired me for this job." Her hands began to shake as fear gripped her heart. Was she being dismissed?

"You are still the cook of the Hampton House." Ellen turned, offering an understanding smile as Olive Hampton strode into the kitchen her skirts swishing with her long strides.

"You need a break Rosa," Olive said softly placing an empty tray on a bare workspace. "I'm not replacing you, and even if you didn't cook, you would have a home here." Olive laid a warm hand on Rosa's arm. "You are part of this family, but you need time to get over what happened."

"No," Rosa said, but there was no real conviction in her word. "I cook."

"Not today," Olive stared the younger woman down. "Today you need to do something different. Take Christina and go for a walk. Hire a buggy and get out of town. Whatever you need, but please rest and deal with whatever it is that is eating you up. You're no good to anyone in your current state."

Rosa lifted her chin stubbornly as fear squirmed in her belly. "I do not wish to go anywhere."

"Then stay in your room all day and play with your little girl. Read a book, take a nap, rest."

Rosa twisted her hands nervously in her apron. If she wasn't working, she would go mad. Too much had happened over the last year and a half, and her emotions were raw. Her heart had been stolen, her world rearranged and the joy that was supposed to last a lifetime had evaporated. "I." She opened her mouth to protest once more, but Shililaih and Arabela joined Olive and all eyes turned on Rosa. There was no anger, nor condemnation in those eyes only determination and compassion.

"Rosa, we all need time to ourselves once in a while. Please rest. We'll take care of everything." Ellen's words were so kind and full of understanding, soothing like a healing balm.

Rosa studied each woman. All were strong, capable, and part of the Hampton family. With these women here, she wasn't needed anymore and fear gnawed at her belly with the thought. If Olive dismissed her how would she care for Christina? How would she feed and shelter her baby girl? She trembled and Olive wrapped an arm around her pulling her close.

"Go," the older woman said. "We'll manage without you for one day. You need this." She held Rosa a moment longer. "Your job is safe," she whispered. "I promise."

Rosa turned, stumbling back toward her room on the back side of the kitchen. She didn't need this. She needed to work. She needed to continue to save the money she had hoarded over the past few months. Without the Hamptons and her job, without the security of work, she would be lost. Olive said her job was safe, but perhaps money was tight with so many mouths to feed. What if she changed her mind or had no choice but to let Rosa go.

An icy shiver rolled down Rosa's spine as she thought back to her mother. Always dependent, always held a hostage in the hands of a deceitful man. Again Rosa shivered as hot tears stung her face. Slipping silently into her room she fell onto the bed burying her face in the pillow and crying with fear, doubt, anger, and despair.

As Rosa silently sobbed out her deepest fears her daughter's soft giggle pulled her from the bed and toward the small crib.

"Oh my sweet girl," Rosa said sitting up and drying her eyes on the hem of her dress. "You will not live the way I did. You will not know the shame, the sorrow of that life."

Rosa stood walking to her daughter's crib and pulling her only child close. Christina rested her still sleepy head on her mother's shoulder and patted Rosa's back with a pudgy hand sending a shock wave of love through the tiny woman.

"My heart," Rosa whispered relishing the feeling of her daughter in her arms. "Perhaps you will be always alone with no brothers or sisters," she sniffed, "but one day you will grow into a beautiful woman, and from now until then, I will do everything to keep you safe."

Christina leaned back placing her little hands on her mother's face and smiling sweetly as she kissed her mother then threw her arms around her once more in a tight hug.

Rosa felt the laughter, long-forgotten bubble up inside her and a sense of wonder filled her. She who had been so unworthy of love had this precious gift. This perfect soul who loved her unconditionally. "Oh, Raul," Rosa sniffed holding her daughter close. "You saw me. You saw past where I had come from and took me to be your wife. I loved you for that, but why, why did you have to get yourself killed?" She felt her heart crumble again. No one would ever know where she had come from, or how Raul had saved her from certain doom with his cheerful nature and big heart.

The big man had made her laugh, promised undying love, and an honorable future and she had grasped it with both hands. Now he was gone, destroyed by his evil brother, and Rosa was alone in a world that treated women as trade goods. She would make Olive understand that she would not lose her temper again. She would not give her a reason to dismiss her. Rosa would not let her daughter suffer the shame and humiliation she had grown up with.

Dressing carefully Rosa prepared Christina and together they walked outside into the cool fresh air of an early Texas morning.

Chapter 8

Dan let his leggy roan amble into town his mind full of thoughts and worries. Needful had been growing steadily, and what had once been a collection of ramshackle shacks and tents now resembled a real cow town.

He smiled as the steady buzz of the sawmill near the creek met his ears and gazed around him at the solid buildings that had sprung up over the past two years.

The Hampton House stood stark, straight and respectable, the heavy timbers of the facade only beginning to darken and weather under the hot Texas sun.

Turning his head he glimpsed the edge of the large livery stable that Orville had built to accommodate stagecoach horses and visiting guest's mounts. Darwin had become an upstanding hostler, and now with his new wife, things were taking on a brighter shine for the man.

Dan scowled as the jailhouse came into sight, sighing as he watched his brother push another drunken cowboy through the door. Needful was still new and many of the younger men, feeling restless and bored, drank too much. Many of his cowpokes had spent a night in the cells of the sheriff's office. There had been too much activity of late in those cells as far as Dan was concerned and his mind shifted to how to curb the problems of the growing town. He barely noticed as the general store, church, and music shop came into view until the familiar petite form of Rosa Rodriguez caught his eye.

***

Rosa jingled the small purse in her hands thinking ahead to what she wanted at the general store. She seldom bought anything not essential for herself or Christina, and since room and board were provided by the Hamptons for her services, she saved her meager wages, jealously.

Stepping from the boardwalk into the street, Rosa's boot heel caught on the step and she staggered dropping her bag as she struggled to right herself once more. Leaning over she reached for the small velvet satchel only to have it whisked from the dust before her very eyes.

"Give that back," she all but shouted snatching at the bag and the man's hand that held it. "It isn't yours."

"I was just trying to help," Dan's voice rolled over her making the hair on the back of her neck prickle.

"You," she glared. "Why do you bother me? Go away."

"I was riding by when I saw you," Dan offered innocently. "I didn't mean any offense."

Rosa snatched the bag from his hands and turned, striding across the street to escape the man, but his hands grasped her pulling her close as three cowboys galloped by.

"Let go of me!" she yelled, her heart pounding at the near-miss of the reckless riders. She hadn't been paying attention, and if Mr. Gaines hadn't grabbed her, she and Christina could have both been run down, but she wasn't going to thank the scoundrel.

Dan's hands shook as he pulled Rosa and her daughter from harm's way. Why did the woman hate him so? His heart sagged as he remembered it was his fault her husband was dead, and he tried to release her, but before he could let go tiny Christina lunged for him wrapping her arms around his neck and her little fingers in his overly long hair.

He cringed trying to extricate himself from the situation, but the little girl only giggled holding tighter and tugging at his dark locks.

"Christina," Rosa gasped, grabbing at her daughter and pulling only to hear the Mayor of Needful hiss when her daughter wouldn't release his hair.

"Let go," he whispered his blue eyes boring into hers. "I'll walk with you a spell until she decides she's tired of me."

Christina squealed again giving another hard tug on Dan's dark hair and making him cringe.

Rosa's eyes flashed. She didn't want to be seen with the handsome rancher walking through town as if he owned her. Tongues would wag, and she had had enough of that in her lifetime, already.

"You walk behind," she snapped her eyes darting to her daughter in annoyance, wanting nothing more than to snatch her from the man's arms, but who knew how vengeful he might be if she caused him harm. He was the Mayor of Needful, after all, a powerful and wealthy man.

Dan nodded flinching as Christina tangled her fingers deeper. He needed a haircut and would stop by to see if Daliah would cut the dark waves, so this couldn't happen again. A smile tugged at his lips as he remembered the first time he had met tiny Christina and her diminutive mother. The baby had been so small, sick, and listless, but the woman who would soon become his sister-in-law had worked tirelessly to save her life.

"Why aren't you working today?" Dan asked as he trailed behind Rosa snapping his eyes up as they fell on the full swish of her smooth skirts. "I thought you cooked most days."

"Today Olive wishes me to be gone." Rosa dropped her head as doubt and worry assailed her.

"She didn't fire you?" Dan gaped. "Rosa I've told you before you don't have to work. You can have your own place. I'll provide for you and Christina."

Rosa whirled around glaring up at the man and meeting his blue eyes with her blazing black eyes. "I will not take your house, your gifts, and your money!" She shouted waggling a finger in his face. "I am not a mujer mantenida. You will not pay for me. You will not buy my favors. I belong to Jesus Christo, not you!"

Rosa rose on her tiptoes, grasped her daughter firmly around the middle, and pulled as Christina began to cry coming away with fistfuls of dark brown hair while her mother raced down the street and away from the man.

Dan Gaines stood stark still on the street, his scalp prickling, as he stared after the woman while she fled. His neck prickled and his scalp stung, but he stood like a poleaxed steer wondering what had just happened.

"Dan," a familiar voice made him blink, and Dan finally turned to look at his brother. "Why don't you come on over to my place. Daliah would like to see you."

Dan nodded still dumbfounded as Rosa's words

echoed in his head. What had she said? Why had she run from him as if he had said something offensive? He only wanted to help. He only wanted to assuage the guilt that gnawed at him each time he saw the beautiful Rosa. "Masjur mantenida," he whispered rolling the word in his mind. He didn't even know what it meant, but the way she had said it, with such disgust, indicated it wasn't good.

***

Spencer Gaines flicked his eyes toward his younger brother under the brim of his hat and wondered what he should do. Dan looked like he'd been kicked in the gut by a rogue bull and was waiting for the horns to finish him off. His face was pale, his eyes glazed, and his mouth kept working over and over but no sound came out.

He hoped Daliah had the coffee pot on because if Dan ever needed a strong brew this was it. Flicking a glance back under his arm he saw Rosa dash through the door of the General Store and hoped Dan hadn't done anything to upset the woman. Cowboys, miners, and other workers from around Needful had grown accustomed to the fine food the young woman provided at the Hampton House, and if she was upset again, he suspected the food would be next to inedible.

Spencer couldn't help but grin though as he thought of the few men who seemed to have been enjoying the hot dishes that Rosa had produced recently, but he was not one of them and hoped that she would calm down soon if she was going to continue as the chief cook at the boarding house.

"Daliah," he called into the house. "I brought company." Spencer's warm chuckle filled the little house as he hurried toward the kitchen his younger brother stumbling behind him as if in a daze. "I hope you have the coffee on," Spence whispered kissing his lovely wife on the cheek. "I think Dan needs it," he added in a whisper.

Daliah turned worried eyes on her brother-in-law who looked like someone had punched him in the gut.

Chapter 9

Rosa hurried into the town's store her heavy skirts swirling around her ankles in agitation.

"Hello Rosa," Mrs. Scripts called cheerily as she popped up from behind the counter. Like Rosa, Alice Scripts was petite, well, downright short. Still, she stood a good two inches taller than Rosa at her full five-foot-one height. "Did you need something for the Hamptons?" Alice smiled at Rosa waving at Christina, making her smile. "I sent their order over with Trey a few minutes ago."

"No, no." Rosa waved the woman's worries away. "Today I am here for me," she hesitated, looking at her little girl and plucking a few strands of brown hair from between Christina's fingers, "and my daughter."

Alice Scripts' bright smile shone like the sun as she hurried around the counter to take Christina. "She's such a good girl," she gushed. "Let me take her while you look around. Is there anything special you were hoping for?"

Rosa's dark eyes roamed the shelves and tables

of the well-stocked stores and smiled. "You have the chocolate," she said her eyes lighting on a large tin of cocoa powder. "I will want that."

Alice hurried toward the floor to ceiling shelf behind the counter reaching for a stick with one hand as she placed Christina on the floor. With a deft flick of her wrist, she plucked the tin from the shelf above her catching it in her other hand. "What else?" she giggled, her brown eyes twinkling.

For the first time in days, Rosa laughed, the soft tinkle of sound bubbling out of her and washing away much of the anger and resentment she felt for Dan Gaines. She felt strong, independent, and capable as she jingled her few coins together in the velvet bag.

"I think I will make a new dress for my daughter," Rosa nodded toward the rack of fabrics her hands stroking a lovely pink and white calico.

"I don't think that would suit her color," Alice said kindly. "What about this?" The storekeeper hurried around the counter leading the toddler toward her mother. "I have a lovely yellow that would look wonderful with Christina's dark hair."

Rosa looked at the fabric and nodded liking the deep butter gold with tiny red daisies scattered about on the soft fabric. If she made it a little too big the child could wear it for at least a year.

"Yes, I think this is good," she agreed, smiling

softly at Alice. "I will take it."

Alice Scripts lifted the bolt of fabric and spread it across the counter, grabbing her scissors and cutting it to length as Rosa walked around the store. Alice liked Rosa and appreciated that she had someone so close to her size in Needful, it made her feel less conspicuous. There was something about the young Mexican woman that spoke of old sorrow and recent loss, and it touched the storekeeper's heart.

She had seen how Daniel Gaines looked at the woman, how his blue eyes filled with confusion, hope, fear, and guilt each time they met. No matter what Dan and Rosa thought of the situation there was more to this story than met the eye. Alice had been a shopkeeper her whole life and was a keen study of human nature. Only time would tell how this tale would end, and Alice prayed it wouldn't be with more heartache and pain.

"Rosa, would you like to join me for a cup of coffee?" Alice asked as she bundled the fabric into brown-paper.

"No," Rosa looked up and smiled at Alice. "I will buy two of those cookies though," she added seeing them on a small plate. "I will take Christina for a day outside."

Alice smiled wrapping the cookies and raising her hand to tell Rosa to wait as she rushed back through a door behind her. "No charge for the cookies or this," Alice beamed stepping out with a small basket in her hands. "I made up some wagon train lemonade earlier and there's a jar inside. You just bring the basket back when you're ready."

Rosa looked between the storekeeper and the basket for several long seconds before finally nodding. She would trust that the other woman didn't want anything from her for the treat. It was so hard to trust even after all of these years, but at some point, she needed to start.

***

Rosa spread the blanket she had found in Alice's basket on the ground by the slow-moving stream then pulled out the cookies and sweet, tangy drink made with vinegar and sugar. Beside her, Christina toddled toward a daisy that swayed in the wind and Rosa smiled.

The fresh air and sunshine spilled over her, warming her to her soul, and she thought back to days when she and Raul had found a quiet moment outdoors between hard work and worried cares.

Birds sang in the branches of an old oak that hung over the water, Spanish moss trailing nearly to the ground on branches that reached toward the earth. It was peaceful, quiet, and restful, and Rosa found herself breathing deeply as tension oozed from her neck and spine.

Christina giggled her pudgy hands reaching for a

butterfly that landed on her flower only to flutter away as the little girl lunged.

Rosa laughed watching her daughter turn to follow the butterfly with her dark eyes. Christina was her joy even on the worst days and reminded her so much of her laughing Raul.

The sound of a horse approaching made Rosa spin racing to scoop up her daughter as she wheeled toward the impending threat.

"It's only me Rosa," Dan drawled wearily. "I didn't mean to disturb you."

Rosa felt some of the tension leave as she lowered her squirming child to the ground. "You startled me," she said watching the man warily. "I thought I was alone."

"I was headed home," Dan said his voice soft. "I saw movement and wasn't sure…" He shrugged leaning forward to rest his elbows on his saddle horn. "I wanted to make sure that everything was all right."

"Why?" Rosa said lifting her chin. "I am not your concern."

"Everyone in Needful is my concern," Dan retorted. "I'm the mayor, and though I never wanted the job, I take it seriously. You may not want me to look out for you, but that's exactly what I'm going to do." The man's horse sidestepped nervously as his emotions translated through the saddle forcing him to rein the animal in.

"Up! Up!" Christina toddled toward the nervous horse and the red roan rolled his eyes as the child approached.

"Christina!" Rosa cried rushing toward her and spooking the horse more.

Dan Gaines bit back a harsh word as his mount reared, diving from the saddle to snatch the child from under the horse's feet. "Whoa, whoa," he soothed bringing the child to where the cowpony could see her. "Easy boy," he said letting his mount stretch its muzzle toward the little girl.

"Be careful," Rosa chided frozen in mid-stride as her heart pounded in her ears.

"I am being careful," Dan growled. "She wasn't in any danger until you lunged toward me," he said forcing his voice into a neutral tone.

Rosa crossed her arm over her middle and glared at the cowboy but didn't speak. He had risked his neck to see that Christina was safe, and she grudgingly admitted that her actions had been foolish.

Dan let Christina pat his pony's nose then hefted her into the saddle, holding her steady with one hand as she squealed with delight.

"See she's fine." Dan turned his face toward Rosa, his smile faltering at her harsh glare. Pulling the little girl from the saddle he turned, letting his horse go and carried the child to her mother. "She's fine Rosa."

Rosa took Christina from him setting her on the blanket and handing her a cookie.

"I do not need you to watch over me or my child," Rosa said. "She is all I have. Do not think I cannot take care of her."

"You could have so much more," Dan said stripping his hat from his head and running a hand through his hair. "I could take care of you provide for you."

"No." Rosa snarled. "I will not be a woman like that. You may be powerful, wealthy, and respected by the people of this town, but you have no right to ask me. I know how men like you are. You say you want nothing then you come in the night, quiet, lonely, and you ask. You take back for the food you give, the house you pay for. I will not be that kind of woman."

"What?" Dan blinked at Rosa trying to understand what she was saying. He wanted nothing from her. His face paled as her words sank in. She thought he wanted her favor for a home and his mouth fell open in shock. What had he ever done to make her think so little of him? "I never," he stammered. "Raul was my friend," his middle gurgled with acid as something in the back of his brain appraised Rosa's lovely face and sultry form. "I'm not," he paused again unable to find the words. "No." Dan exploded storming back to his horse and throwing himself into the saddle as he raked the roan with cruel spurs as he sped away.

Rosa scowled after the retreating form as his horse charged across the prairie. He had seemed startled at her words as if he hadn't known what she would say.

She had known men like him before, and though confused by his odd behavior, would not soften toward him or his offer. Her own father had seemed like a good respectable man, but time had proven otherwise as she had grown to know exactly who he was.

Returning to the blanket with her daughter, Rosa put the troublesome man from her mind and reached for a cookie smiling and speaking to her baby girl in fluent Spanish as the day trudged on.

Chapter 10

Dan dragged his heaving pony to a sliding stop outside the barn, dropped from the saddle, and stormed toward his home. His heart dipping from anger to shock and back again as he slammed through the front door bellowing for coffee.

Old Cookie stepped from the kitchen and scowled. His boss was usually an even-tempered sort of man, but woman troubles always did cloud a man's brain.

"Stop your bellerin'," the old man snapped pointing to a chair as he turned to the big stove. "Coffee's on already."

Dan dropped into a chair dropping his head into his hands with a groan. How had Rosa thought he had anything but honorable intentions? Didn't she understand that he felt responsible for what happened to Raul and only wanted to help?

"Here's your dad-blamed coffee," the old man snapped. "Are ya done catter-wallin' or should I leave ya be?"

"Huh?" Dan lifted his eyes to the old man's

scrunched-up face. "Oh. Sorry Cookie," he said his shoulders sagging as he reached for his cup. "I'm, I'm." He looked up his blue eyes confused. "I don't know what I am."

The old cook grabbed a cup of coffee and pulled a chair in front of his boss. "What happened?" he asked leaning forward and staring the other man down. "Go on, tell old Cookie everything."

Dan sipped his coffee letting the bitter brew blend with his bitter soul. "You won't believe it."

"You'd be surprised what I'd believe," the old man said slurping from his cup. "Go on, I ain't tellin' no one. What's said between a man and his cook stays between 'em."

Dan Gaines chuckled shaking his head.

"She thinks." He swallowed with disgust. "Rosa Rodriguez thinks I want to have her as my kept woman."

The old cook nodded slowly as if this made perfect sense to him and Dan growled. "I never," he blustered. "She's Raul's wife. He was my friend. I just want to help. Keep her safe. See that she and Christina don't go without."

He sounded like a prairie dog barking out a warning to his kin, but he couldn't pull his thoughts together better than that. It felt like someone had placed a vice on his head and that it might crack wide open at any moment.

"She is a mighty attractive woman," the old cook said. "I reckon plenty of men wouldn't mind havin' her as a spicy dish on the side."

Dan sprang to his feet his fist balling before his chair ever hit the floor. "Why you no good, dirty old man!" he shouted.

"Calm down, calm down," Cookie said not even bothering to stand. "I ain't bein' disrespectful just realistic like. She's a pretty woman, and I'm sure plenty of men have noticed." His eyes twinkled. "Even you."

"Cookie, I'm warning you," Dan growled. "Rosa Rodriguez is no one to speak about that way."

"Oh shut up." The cook glared reaching forward and grabbing for Dan's upended chair. "If you're so het up about her reputation and seeing she's cared for, go marry her yourself and be done with it."

Dan staggered back a step, his boot heel catching on his chair as he toppled over hitting the floor with a crash.

Cookie slapped his knee throwing back his head and cackling like a mad man as Dan landed on his backside with a thump.

"I," Dan said still blinking at the man as if he'd sprouted another head. "No."

The old cook stood to his feet, his boots scraping on the floor as he leaned down meeting Dan's hard blue gaze. "Give me one good reason why not?" he snarled. "She's alone. She's single. She's perty." He ticked each thought off on his fingers. "You ain't got no wife," he added dropping his hand and offering it to his boss. "If you marry her, she'll know you ain't got no nefarious designs upon her person." The old man grinned, showing the gaps in his yellowed teeth, delighted with his turn of phrase.

"I do not need a wife." Dan grasped the other man's hand hauling himself back to his feet and righting his chair.

"Then you'd both be perfect for each other. She don't want no one botherin' her or her daughter, and you don't want a wife. You can marry her and put her up in that little old house down by the spring."

Dan gaped at the man in horror, spinning on his heel and stomping from the house.

***

When Rosa returned to the Hampton House at lunchtime she was pleased to see the dining hall full of patrons once more. In the days since her rescue, she had found that there had been fewer customers eating there, and she was relieved to see things closer to normal.

As much as she hated to admit it the troubles she had been through so recently had left her unsettled, worried, and not focused on her cooking.

"There you are," Olive smiled waving her over to a table where she was enjoying a hot corned beef and cabbage meal. "The girls are cooking and don't hardly need me at all," the older woman laughed. "I'm not going to complain though. It's nice to be off my feet for a few minutes."

"Do you want me to serve?" Rosa asked. "You do not need to work so hard. I am here."

"No, you sit and visit with me for a spell," Olive said reaching up for Christina. "Things have been so crazy since the men brought you and Ruth back that I feel like none of us has had a chance to catch our breath. It's why I wanted you to take the day off. Now and again a woman needs a bit of time on her own."

Rosa smiled as relief washed over her. Olive still wanted her to cook and work for her. She had simply wanted to be kind and give her a break. She ducked her head thinking of her disturbed feelings since the rescue. It had been easier to be angry about the incident than to face her response to it.

"Rosa is there something you want to tell me?" Olive asked studying her friend's face. "You've been." The older woman bit her lip then plunged on. "You've been rather upset of late."

Rosa looked up from where she had been plucking at her skirt. "It is not something I wish to speak of," she said with a slight shake of her head. "No one will understand," she added looking around at the men enjoying their meals.

"Well, I'm not one to pry," Olive said her dark eyes seeking any hint of what could be troubling Rosa. "But if you need to talk remember that you have friends here in Needful who love you. Folks who want to help you. Even with Raul gone, you are not alone."

Rosa offered a sad smile feeling her husband's absence once more. Why had he done it? Why had he borrowed from his outlaw brother? She shook her head as she sighed. She needed to forgive Raul. Sooner or later she had to let go of her anger and Raul.

"Thank you, Olive," Rosa spoke so softly Olive almost missed her words. "I will ask if I need help."

Olive smiled. "Good, now what did you buy at the store?" the old woman asked looking at the packages Rosa had placed on the table. "Are we going to have a chance to make something pretty?"

Rosa nodded opening her package and showing the fabric. "I will make a new dress for Christina."

"She will be so pretty in that. It's the perfect color and so cheerful."

Rosa nodded smiling at Ellen who brought her a plate of food and a cup of tea, setting a plate before little Christina and letting Olive feed the child. Perhaps Rosa would calm down enough for things to get back to normal. No one was sure what had set her off again, but they were hoping she would find some peace soon.

Chapter 11

Spencer Gaines watched the dark stranger angle his horse down the main drag of Needful, his watchful eyes taking in the sleek horse, low slung gun belt, and expensive suit. The man came from money whoever he was, and by the cut of his short coat and shiny books, he hailed from south of the border.

"Can I help you?" Spencer asked turning from the wall he had been leaning against and stepping into the street where his tin badge caught the light.

"I am looking for someone." The man's dark eyes raked over Spencer as his carefully clipped and heavily accented words fell around them.

"Someone in trouble?" Spencer asked casually his eyes still pinned on the man's face.

"I am looking for my daughter."

Spencer chuckled but stopped at the man's harsh glare. "I'm sorry," the sheriff of Needful said. "It's just that we had another gentleman ride in recently looking for his daughter as well. Why don't you step down and come inside? I'll see what I can do."

The silver-haired man with the long mustache nodded once easing his high necked horse to the hitching rail and swinging down. "This is acceptable."

Spencer raised a brow as the man hitched his horse to the rail. The lone rider was obviously from money and was used to people doing what he said. His thick Spanish accent hinted at old money from Mexico and Spencer hoped he wouldn't be trouble for the tiny town. They had already had enough of that to go around for a while.

"You have been the sheriff of this town for a long time?" the older man followed Spencer into his office his dark eyes taking in everything.

"Not too long," Spencer admitted closing the door behind them and shutting out the curious gazes of those making their way through Needful. The afternoon was still quiet, and Spencer couldn't help but hope it stayed that way, but something told him that this man's arrival would surely bring changes to Needful, for good or ill was yet to be determined.

***

Dan ran. The ranch owner dashed from his own home grabbed the first horse he saw and threw a leg over.

"Hey!" the cowboy, who had been preparing to mount up, yelled as the boss took off with the horse he had just saddled.

"What's his problem," the cowboy asked looking to Dozer, but the rancher was already fanning it across the plains in search of peace and quiet.

The wind whipped past Dan's face as he galloped in no particular direction at all. He was angry, confused and guilt rode his shoulders raking him with glinting spurs. The fresh mount pounded across the prairie, head down and ears flat as if the devil himself was hot on their trail and Dan thought maybe he was. If only he had known about Raul's troubles, things would have been all right and now the voices ricocheting around his head were making his temples pound.

Charging down a hill his cowhand instincts kicked in and he leaned back, pulling the pony's head in and sliding down the hill in a shower of dust, sagebrush, and wildflowers before hitting the flat plain still at a dead run.

A deep rumble bubbled from Dan's chest and he started laughing, pulling the foaming horse into a walk at the bottom of the hill. It had been a wild ride, but he knew he couldn't outrun the real problems pounding in his brain.

Slacking his reins, he let the horse wander as its breathing eased and the prairie breeze began to dry glistening flanks. The horse had been fast, sure-footed and brave, never hesitating to leap where his rider guided.

Again the cowboy chuckled naming himself for the fool he was. He could have broken his neck racing across the rugged range like that, but for some reason, he was still in one piece and needed to deal with the problem at hand.

Letting his horse amble, head drooping toward the glistening pool that marked the headwaters of the stream that ran through his property, Dan sighed. Inside a little voice seemed to accuse, nattering at him until he couldn't deny it anymore. He cared for Rosa Rodriguez. He was attracted to the wife of the man who had worked loyally for him over the past few years, and the taste of betrayal rose in his throat like hot bile.

How could he possibly feel this way for another man's wife? He hadn't planned on having any feelings for Rosa, but the stark truth stared back at him with glimmering black eyes.

The pony dipped its head kicking dust and rocks into the pool as it sucked greedily at the cool water. Dan let the reins run through his hand so the horse could drink and gazed around him at his land.

So many things had changed since he and his men had first arrived in the town of Needful. Dan's loud snort made his pony jump and he eased it back to the pool soothing the big bay with hand and word. When he'd arrived on this particular patch of prairie, the town of Needful didn't exist. Only a small trading post and a few diggers even knew of the area.

No the town of Needful hadn't even had a name until Olive Hampton had blurted out that it needed just about everything to even be called a town. He had built a ranch with the few men who had followed him from the war-ravaged east and sought solace in this wide-open land.

Dan hung his head in shame as guilt gnawed at him like a pack of hungry rats. He had called Raul a friend from the moment he had met the jovial Mexican. The large man with a big belly and a bigger laugh had signed on with Dan to wrangle cows, build structures and translate when more of his people came looking for jobs.

Wanting to add to his growing herd, Dan had used Raul for trips across the border to trade for stock, equipment, and mounts while Rosa and their baby stayed behind cooking for the men of Needful from a small tent in the heart of town.

Raul had been a hard worker, determined to provide for the small family he had brought with him from a small dirt farm that hadn't panned out in Mexico. They had come seeking a new life and had found work, even friendship in Needful.

Dan had trusted the big man with the bright

easy smile and had begun letting him help others in the area navigate the difficult trading routes of the Texas-Mexican border. If he had known that Raul had borrowed money from his outlaw brother, he would have been happy to advance the money to his friend possibly saving his life. Raul had been as proud as he had been cheerful, and that pride had cost him his life.

"Why?" Dan wondered looking up as the pink light of the setting sun spread, like blood across the prairie as bright stars began to twinkle to life. "Why?"

The pony had drunk its fill and shifted snatching mouthfuls of grass along the bank, but Dan simply sat there staring off into the darkening sky as he fought the feelings rising in his breast.

He never intended to betray his friend. In the past, he hadn't seen Rosa as anything, but the wife of a man he trusted, but now, as the darkness of night descended like a silent shroud around him he had to admit his determination to protect and care for Rosa and Christine had become something more.

Dan slipped from his horse's back holding the reins in his hands as he bent splashing cool water on his face and drying it with his bandana. He didn't know what to do, and with Rosa's misunderstanding of his intentions, he wasn't even sure he could do anything about them if he tried.

Old Cookie's mad notion of marrying her was the craziest thing he had ever heard, but just maybe it could work.

Dan shook his head as something slithered through the water unnoticed by him until his horse reared ripping the reins through his hands in a hard burn before knocking him in the dirt as it plunged into the night leaving him alone to watch the black rattler slither from the water and coil around a dark bush.

***

Rosa fluffed the pillows in one of the rooms and turned to study her handiwork. It was odd not cooking again today, but being alone with her thoughts hadn't helped either.

She was still furious with the Mayor of Needful and irritated with everyone in the town who couldn't see what a terrible man he was as well.

"Rosa, are you just about done in there?" Olive called as she opened the door. "The stage should be here in another hour or so, and I don't know what we should expect yet. I suppose that once the railroad reaches Needful, we'll have even more guests or at least folks stopping to rest a spell." Olive came to a stop, meeting Rosa's dark eyes. "I wish you'd tell me what's bothering you."

"You would not believe what I would say." Rosa's dark eyes studied Olive's face and she wished she could tell her friend. She wished she could pour out everything without then seeing the look of disgust that would change her friend's opinion of her forever. Rosa knew all too well what it felt like to have others look down on her.

Raul had never looked at her like that. Never put her down or believed less of her for what her mother was.

Olive grasped Rosa's hand, making her sit on the bed with her and giving her a harsh look. "Rosa, you are my friend, and ever since you were brought home, you've been in a snit. You have made food so spicy most men can't eat it, thrown a pot of stew at our mayor, and generally been impossible to live with. Now I love you, but it is time you explain what is going on."

Rosa sagged, feeling the weariness that had plagued her ever since she had lost Raul. He had only been trying to look out for her, but look at what it had cost.

"If I tell you, you will not want me here anymore," Rosa sighed. "Where will I go? What will I do?"

Olive turned to face the petite woman willing her to meet her gaze. "Rosa you are as much a part of this family as any of my sons, their wives, or their children. What in the world could make me see you any other way? Now tell me. Please."

Rosa stiffened her spine, folded her hands in

her lap, and turned to look Olive directly in the eye. "My mother never married my father." She watched studying the boarding housekeeper's face but saw only curiosity. "We, my brothers and I, we are what you say, love children. We are…"

Olive laid her hand over Rosa's. "I understand," she said. "You don't have to use that word. But I still don't see what that has to do with anything."

Rosa's cheeks flushed with anger as she thought of her situation. "I am angry because Mayor Dan wants to put me in a house on his ranch the way my father kept my mother. I will not do it." She sprang to her feet taking a turn around the small room. "I am not that kind of woman. Raul. Raul knew about my family, and he did not care. He brought us here to America where we could have a new life with none of the past following, but now this man that everyone loves and respects…" she paused her eyes flashing and heart pounding. "Now this Dan Gaines thinks he will make me the same!"

"Rosa, you can't believe this?" Olive said standing and feeling the blood drain from her face. "Mayor Dan isn't that kind of man. I'm sure you misunderstood."

Rosa shook her head. "No." she slashed her hand downward in irritation. "He says he will give me a house, take care of me and Christina, but I know how this is. My father, he was a well-respected man in our town. He had power, wealth, influence, and he kept my mother for her favors. He bought us pretty gifts and sat with us when he would visit, but always he would go home to his wife and family. There are men like this in the world. They hide behind a glaze of respectability always fooling those who do not want to look too close. I will not be fooled. I will not do this thing."

Olive twisted her hands in her apron, her nerves jangling as she listened to Rosa. Surely the young woman was mistaken. Mayor Dan only wanted to help take care of her because Raul was his friend. With a successful cattle ranch and his other responsibilities to the town, he was only thinking of looking after Rosa and her little girl. Wasn't he?

"Rosa, I'm sure you're mistaken," Olive said softly. "But either way you do not need to ever leave the Hampton House. You have a home here as long as you want, and it doesn't even matter if you cook. You are like a daughter to me," she finished pulling Rosa in for a tight hug. "Me and Orville we love you and that tiny mite of yours is a piece of our heart. Don't you think a thing about this anymore." Olive released Rosa tipping her head and studying her closely. "What I don't understand though is why you're in such a snit now. Dan's been talking at you for months, so what happened that set you off?"

Rosa looked up at her friend tipping her chin in irritation. "He kissed me!" she spat with all the venom of a sidewinder gone mad.

Chapter 12

Dan didn't move, didn't breathe, didn't dare to twitch, as the long lithe form of the fat-bodied rattler curled in the dust. The snake didn't seem to have noticed him yet, and if it would just move on, he would get out of the way as fast as possible, but for now, the snake's golden eyes glinted in the dull gleam of the moon as its tongue danced over the dirt sniffing for prey.

Closing his eyes he lifted a silent prayer to God begging for grace and forgiveness for his foolish race into the wilds. He deserved whatever happened to him at this point for his headlong charge across the Texas Prairie. He had been a fool to leave like that.

The telltale sound of the snake's rattle vibrated making Dan's heart all but stop beating in his breast. Quick as lightening the snake lunged in a flash of fangs and whip-like body but instead of sinking lethal venom-filled points into the cowboy, it darted to the side grasping a small gray mouse while Dan dove the other way rolling across the dirt, brush, and cactus of the grasslands. In one move he was on his feet and turning back toward the town he had left a short time ago. That was too close for comfort, and he had things he needed to do. A particularly stubborn woman's face flashed before his eyes and his heart kicked into overtime with the rush of adrenaline and heat. He had escaped the rattlesnake, but what was he to do about Rosa?

No answer came to mind immediately and Dan chuckled, the sound merging with the yip of a coyote somewhere in the night. Perhaps he didn't know what he was going to do about Rosa and the war of emotion battling in his heart, but he had a nice, long, slow walk home to think about it.

Settling into a slow steady gait, Dan Gaines turned toward Needful. He was closer to the town than his ranch and with the bright clear sky dazzling above, he chose his path and set out. He was bound to take a good deal of abuse from his riders about riding out and losing his horse, but right now the problem of Rosa Rodriguez was what plagued his mind.

How could she have ever thought that he wanted to... He stopped that train of thought as images of her in a little house near his home flashed through his mind. She was a beautiful woman, warm and spirited but she was his friend's wife.

Dropping his head Dan sighed. There was no easy answer to the problem. Rosa thought he was a scoundrel. Cookie told him to marry her, and he didn't know what to think. "Confound it, Raul, why did you have to go and get yourself killed."

A bright star twinkled in the sky, and Dan remembered back to meeting the smiling man a few years earlier. He hadn't even known about Rosa at the time. Then when he found out that Raul had a wife and daughter, he had offered him a place at the ranch, but the man refused to have them move to the ranch.

Would it be so wrong to think of Rosa as more than his dead friend's wife? Could he provide for her, make up for his mistakes, by marrying her? None of it made any sense at all, and he was no closer to figuring it out as the night cooled, and he pulled his light jacket around him.

If Rosa wouldn't accept his offer to provide for her, perhaps he could do something for the Hamptons to ensure she never had to look for another job.

Kicking his boot in the dirt he gazed around him at the empty landscape. Though the darkness obscured it, the prairie teamed with life, and he knew that animals, birds, and insects were even now going about their business of living.

The chill of the night crept down his spine and he finally faced the thought he had been avoiding for so long. Why? Why had he kissed Rosa when they had rescued her from her evil brother-in-law?

They had ridden into the camp, Darwin Rivers at the lead, with a blazing pistol in his hand. Fear, doubt, worry had washed over Dan in a wave and then when the last outlaw was lying on the ground he had swept Rosa into his arms and kissed her as relief carried him away.

It didn't make sense. He wasn't a man given to moods or outbursts. Between him and Spencer, he would say he had always been the more level headed, serious type. It was what led him to the rank of Captain during the war. His quiet calculation of every situation had carried him and his men through many scrapes and out again. So why had it been so different this time?

Something warm wriggled in Dan's gut, but he squelched it, ignoring the whisper breathed into his soul as his heart tried to reply.

It had been the excitement, the danger. That was what had caused him to react the way he had, and now with Rosa's accusations, he had to figure out what to do. What kind of man did she think he was that she believed him capable of having a woman on the side?

He wasn't much interested in marriage or a family, at least not at this point, but he wouldn't even consider a situation like the one she had described.

Shaking his head the cowboy didn't see the prairie dog hole until he'd stumbled over it twisting his ankle and he sat down hard pulling his booted foot up onto his other leg. He had never wanted to blast his luck so badly in his life as he sat in the cold prairie alone and confused while the coyotes howled at a waxing moon and the wind skittered through the dry grasses like a lovers sigh.

He didn't know how long he sat there listening to the wind and watching the night sky, but the air danced around him, teasing him with soft kisses and his heart began to sink.

Had there been more to the kiss than he would let himself believe? Shaking his head, he was sure it had been the overwhelming relief, but what about what his old cook had said? Could he give Rosa the security he owed her if he married her? Would she agree to a marriage in name only? The thoughts whirled through his head like a maelstrom, and he didn't know which direction to go.

Flopping back on the dry grass Dan gazed up at the heavens. "God, I don't know what I'm supposed to do," he mused. "I'm just a rancher. I never wanted any of this, but here I am stuck in this mess and not sure what end is up. Show me what you want me to do, and if you don't mind, make it mighty clear. When it comes to cows, wranglers, and town business I seem to be alright, but when there's a woman involved, I can't make hide nor hair of the whole mess. Whatever you want of me I'll do it to keep Rosa and Christina safe." Dan let the prayer hang on the night wind for long minutes as doubt assailed him then lifted his eyes once more to the sparkling stars above. "Amen." He spoke firmly trusting that what he was supposed to do would be revealed. His eyes growing heavy, he eased his pistol on his hip, tucked a rock under his head and let sleep find him. Tomorrow would be soon enough to face the problems of the day.

***

"Hey boss man," a droll voice startled Dan as the first rays of the morning sun brushed the horizon. "You decide your bed ain't good enough for you no more?" Teddy Lewis chuckled as he let his horse lean over and sniff at Dan's hat.

"You're going to be on permanent drag duty if you don't watch it," Dan growled back grabbing his hat and shoving it on his head as he sat up.

Teddy just laughed, his usually serious dark eyes, twinkling with mirth.

"Give me a hand up," Dan said reaching for the younger man's hand. "I twisted my ankle coming back last night."

Teddy offered the boss his hand helping him swing up behind the saddle.

"Home or town?" the young man asked.

Dan looked down at his dusty coat and gritty hands. "Town," he mumbled. He'd stop at Spencer's and let Daliah check his ankle while Teddy fetched him a horse.

"You're the boss," Teddy drawled with a laugh turning his horse toward Needful and making Dan groan. It was going to be a long time before anyone let him live this down.

"Anything happen while I've been out wandering the wilds on my own?" Dan asked.

"Not that I've heard," Teddy said. "I'll drop you at Spence's place," he added with a grin. "You want me to fetch a horse from the ranch or just get Darwin to saddle you a livery nag?"

Dan shook his head. "You go on back to the

ranch and let everyone know I'm not dead. I'll get a horse at the livery when I'm done in town."

"I can't wait to tell the boys about this," Teddy laughed. "The Mayor of Needful got himself lost on the prairie not five miles from town."

***

"Daliah," Dan called as he hobbled into the neat little house behind the jail a while later. "Daliah are you here?"

"Dan, what are you doing here?" Daliah stepped from a tiny kitchen drying her hands on a towel and eyeing his rumpled appearance. "And what did you do to your ankle?" she added taking his arm and helping him to a chair.

"Oh, I let my horse wander off last night then stepped in a prairie dog hole," Dan grumbled. "I'm sure it's nothing, but if you'd take a look." His blue eyes met her dark gaze noting the smile that tugged at her lips. "Where's Spencer?"

"He's talking to a man who rode into town yesterday. He's from down south, and says he's looking for his daughter."

"Another one?" Dan asked in shock. "Don't tell me Olive has another young woman over at the Hampton House who ran off without telling her folks?"

"Not that I know of," Daliah laughed tugging on his boot. "Sorry," she said when he flinched. "It's either this or cut the boot off."

"No, I'll live. Besides I just got these boots broke in," he laughed wincing again as she gave the boot a hard tug pulling it free.

Daliah's hands were cool as she rolled his sock down and looked at the swollen bruising around his ankle and foot. "Looks like a sprain," she said. "It should be alright, but you need to stay off of it for a couple of days. If possible get it into an ice bath to bring the swelling down."

Dan laughed. "I don't see that happening anytime soon with it almost the end of summer."

"No, I suppose not. It would be nice to have an icebox or even an icehouse here, but it is usually just too warm, even in winter. Let me wrap this ankle then I'll walk you over to the Hampton House. I think we'll find Spencer there."

Dan nodded. It was nice having a sister-in-law who knew about healing. Maybe Needful didn't have a doctor, but Daliah was nearly as good as any sawbones he had ever met.

"Do you know who this man is?" He asked as Daliah pulled heavy strips of cloth from a cupboard. "Who his daughter is?"

"No," Daliah admitted wrapping his ankle with care. "I guess we'll find out when we meet him."

The sound of a galloping horse had Dan springing to his feet again and peering out the window of his brother's home as Teddy slid to a stop in front of the Sherriff's office.

"Teddy, what are you doing back?" Dan called hopping out onto the small front porch. "I thought I sent you home."

"I was on my way Dan," the younger man said but as I rode out, I came across a bunch of rough lookin' men camped along the road. I thought I should let Spence know just in case they were plannin' to do something bad."

"I'll get Spencer," Dan said hobbling back into the house searching for his boot. "You ride out and keep an eye on those men."

"Yes sir," Teddy barked scrabbling back into the saddle.

"And keep out of sight," Dan yelled after him as he shot Daliah a troubled glance. "Where d'you say Spencer is?" he asked his blue eyes worried.

Chapter 13

"No!" Rosa's voice, raised in anger, floated out the boarding house door and Dan charged forward ignoring the lancing pain in his ankle.

"No!" Rosa's word came again quieter but no less vehemently. "I will not go with you. This is my home and I will stay."

"Rosalita," a well-dressed man with a thick mustache spoke. His voice was soft but rang with authority as if he were used to being obeyed. "You have no husband. No one to protect you, provide for you and your daughter. You will come home."

"No," Rosa placed her hands on her hips and glared up at the man her dark eyes flashing with anger. "I am not some cow or horse for you to come and collect. I have a job here, and I will stay." Rosa carefully spoke each word forcing herself to use English so that those around her could understand. "You have no right to tell me what to do."

"You are being stubborn," the man said and Dan froze, Daliah nearly bumping into him as he watched from the dark doorway of the Hampton House. "I will provide for you, protect you. Think of what happened to you so recently. Do not think that I have not heard of Raul's death or his brother's behavior. You could have been killed. What would have become of your child then?"

Rosa visibly paled at the man's words, but she didn't back down, and Dan couldn't help but grin as the tiny woman glared back at the man before her.

"I was in no danger," Rosa said lifting her chin as her nostrils flared. "Rivera did not want to harm me. He wanted me to cook." Rosa's loud snort was one of the most unladylike things he had ever seen Rosa do, but he grinned anyway. The woman had fire and was not backing down under the onslaught of reasoning from the obviously wealthy man.

"You will come home." The older man said crossing his arms over his chest. "You are my daughter, and you will return to your home where I can protect and provide for you."

Rosa was visibly trembling now, her hands curled into fists at her side as she rose on the tips of her boot toes. "The way you protected and provided for my mother." Rosa's word sent a chill down Dan's back. This softer, quieter tone was deadly compared to her angry shouting from a moment ago.

Across the room, Dan caught his brother's eye

and the slight shake of Spencer's head held him in his place.

"You do not own me," Rosa continued her voice a breathy hiss. "I will not come home to be auctioned off to the highest bidder when the mood strikes you. You kept my mother on a string, but I will not be trapped. I will not be treated like a common..."

Before the next word slipped from her lips the older man raised his hand and Rosa reeled back in fear.

"You will not say this about your mother," the man barked his dark eyes flashing with fury, as he lowered his hand to his side. "She was a good woman."

Rosa snorted and the man leaned forward meeting her harsh gaze. "You do not know this," he snarled. "You were gone by then, but I married your mother before she died. I found good matches for your brothers and sisters, and I will do the same for you." Quick as lightning, the man's hand shot out grasping Rosa's arm pulling her to him. "You will come with me. I am your father, and I have spoken."

Dan straightened his spine and sauntered to the middle of the room a bright grin on his face as he slipped an arm around Rosa pulling her close and placing a kiss on her cheek. "Hello darlin'," he drawled the smile still on his face. "Who's this?

Did he come for the wedding?"

Rosa wheeled turning to stare at Dan's face and sucked in a breath as he winked at her still grinning like a fool.

"Dan Gaines," the cowboy said offering the man his hand. "Mayor of Needful at your service."

Flashing a glance at Rosa the man turned to face Dan dropping the young woman's arm and reaching for the cowboy's extended hand. "Juan Xavier Hernandez," the man offered tipping his head slightly. "I have come to take my daughter home."

Dan shook the man's hand keeping the grin plaster on his face as he assessed the situation. "Rosa," he said dropping Juan's hand and tightening his arm around Rosa's shoulders. "You didn't tell me your father was coming. Did you send him an invitation? Surely he understands you can't leave now. Not with our wedding only days away."

Rosa slipped out from under Dan's arm turning to look at him, her eyes confused, but before she could speak, he leaned in pecking her on the lips and then turned his head to whisper in her ear. "Play along. I promise it will be alright."

Rosa leaned back her dark eyes studying Dan's face for a moment before she took a deep breath and slipped his arm around her once more.

"I did not invite my father," she said snuggling under Dan's arm and slipping into his heart. "I do not need him here for my wedding day. He was not there for my first one. I do not need him now."

"You are the mayor of this town?" Juan Xavier asked looking to the sheriff for confirmation. "You say you are marrying my daughter, but she did not mention this."

"Well I only just convinced her to take me," Dan chuckled turning Rosa deftly with his hand at her waist. "Why don't we have a seat, and we'll talk a bit." He gestured toward an empty table grinning as he pulled out a chair for Rosa and nodded toward Spencer. "I'll just be a minute," Dan leaned in kissing Rosa's cheek once more. "I need to tell Spencer something."

Spencer nodded taking Dan's hint and following him toward the door.

"What on earth are you doing?" Spence growled as soon as they were out of earshot, looking at his brother as if he had lost his mind.

"I don't have time right now," Dan said his eyes darting back to Rosa where she sat glaring at the man across the table from her. "Teddy just rode in while Daliah was tending my ankle and said there's a pack of hard looking men camped out along the road. I sent him out to keep an eye on them, but you might want to check on them."

Spencer nodded. "I think they are Juan Xavier's men," Spencer said turning to look at the older man. "I hope you know what you're doing."

"So do I," Dan hissed. "It's plain to see Rosa doesn't want anything to do with that man, and if she doesn't want to go, she doesn't have to. I'll do whatever it takes to make sure she has a say in her life."

Spencer flashed his eyes toward Daliah who simply smiled back at him her dark eyes holding secrets even he couldn't comprehend. "Let me talk to Mr. Hernandez," he offered. "After that, you're on your own. I hope you aren't getting over your head."

Dan nodded plastering the ridiculous grin on his face once more and turning toward the table. "It's all settled," Dan's words didn't put a dent in the chill that hung at the small table. "Spence agreed to be my best man, but first he has to ride out to see about some fella's camped down the road."

Mr. Hernandez turned giving Spencer a quick nod. "Those will be my vaqueros." The man's voice was soft but rang with authority. "They are of no concern to you."

"I'd like to decide that for myself," Spencer said his blue eyes studying the other man. "It's my job as sheriff of Needful."

"Very well," Juan reached into the pocket of his dark coat and pulled out a note pad and pencil. "Give this note to Manuel. Tell them to make themselves comfortable, and I will come soon."

Spencer waited patiently while the man wrote the note then handed it to him. "I'll be back soon," he said nodding at Dan who had slipped into a chair next to Rosa. "I wouldn't want to miss anything important."

***

Daliah's light laughter made Spencer skid to a halt on the other side of the front door as he tried to collect his thoughts.

"This should be interesting," his lovely wife said reaching out and taking his hand.

"I'm not sure I follow," he said leaning into her. When Spencer had met Daliah, he knew that she was the last thing he needed in his life, but it turned out she was just the thing he couldn't live without.

"Dan and Rosa," Daliah grinned. "He's been dancing around the real issue for months, and now it is staring him right in the face."

"Honey, I'm not sure what you're on about, but I need to ride out and make sure these men aren't going to be a problem. If nothing else, having a group like that around after what happened with Rivera and his gang will make people nervous."

Daliah rolled her eyes taking Spencer's other hand and pulling him closer as she gazed into his dazzling blue eyes. "Dan and Rosa." She shook her head. "Don't you see?"

"See what?"

Daliah's laugh washed over him, and he couldn't help but grin even if he wasn't sure what she was talking about.

"Your brother is in love with Rosa, but he hasn't even realized it himself. He's so worked up about what happened to Raul that he hasn't seen what's in his own heart."

Spencer blinked at his beautiful wife shaking his head slowly. "He just wants to help," he insisted. "He feels responsible for what happened to Raul."

"And he feels guilty for how attracted he is to Rosa when she was the wife of his friend."

"Daliah don't you think you're being fanciful?" Spencer asked. He knew his wife to be a sensible woman, kind, caring, and talented in the healing arts, but women could get romantic notions sometimes too.

"No," She replied tipping up and kissing his lips. "You mark my words; Dan really will do whatever it takes to give Rosa her freedom." Daliah laughed softly again. "Even if he has to marry her."

Spencer turned looking back at the closed door to the eatery and shook his head as Dan's words filled his mind once more. "Is this a good thing or a bad thing?"

"Only time will tell," Daliah grinned.

Spencer glanced around him then leaned in for another quick kiss before resting his forehead against Daliah's. "I have a feeling this whole mess is going to give me headaches," he admitted.

"I'll mix the willow bark then," Daliah laughed. "Now go see about these men and come home. I'll make us lunch."

Chapter 14

Dan sat across from the man who claimed to be Rosa's father as waves of hostility radiated from the woman next to him.

She had been about to lose her battle with the man only moments ago, and he couldn't let that happen. He knew how proud Rosa was. How she worked hard to provide for herself and her daughter Christina. He couldn't let this man charge in and whisk her away if she didn't want to go.

Thanking Shi, one of Olive and Orville's daughters-in-law, for the coffee she placed before them, he studied Mr. Hernandez waiting to see what the man would do next.

"Why do you wish to marry my daughter?" the older man asked his dark eyes, so much like Rosa's, glinted with a hard light.

"Why, because I love her," Dan replied with a grin turning to study Rosa who wouldn't meet his eyes. "She's the sunshine in my life," he added as the taste of coffee turned bitter on his tongue.

The words spilling from his lips were said

cheerily but each declaration hit him like a punch to the gut as he realized that they were true.

He had been fighting these feelings for a long time, not truly even understanding what they were. At first, it had been a need to help. A desire to see to it that Raul's widow was taken care of, but as his offers had been met with stubborn obstinacy he had grown to respect the infuriating woman. He hadn't understood why she refused his offer of a little house and a place to live, but now it was clear and his heart melted with the realization that somewhere along the way he had fallen in love with Rosa Rodriguez.

"And you Rosa?" Juan's dark eyes turned to his daughter who looked up with a start.

"I would have nothing less," Rosa said her voice sharp. Slowly she turned to Dan a bright smile flashing across her soft features. "Mr. Gaines is a good man. He is well respected in Needful and will make a good husband."

Dan managed to stop himself from flinching as the word husband dropped from her lips but was too startled by her hand twining with his to speak.

"I do not need you here father," Rosa continued. "I am an independent woman who has chosen to marry well. You can go home to Mexico. You do not need to worry about your little Rosalita."

"Go home?" Mr. Hernandez laughed. "When my

daughter is getting married? No, no, no. I missed your first wedding. I will not miss this one." The older man pushed himself to his feet. "I will pay for the best wedding this town has ever seen. You will have the wedding your mother never could."

Smiling the man doffed his hat and stepped away from the table, pausing to turn back to the gaping couple. "You may not believe me, Rosa," he spoke softly, "but I loved your mother. I would have married her sooner if possible. My wife, her family was wealthy, powerful; I would have lost everything if I had left her. When she died, I went to your mother begging her to be my wife, but she insisted that we wait a respectable time. I was young and foolish when I first wed. I would have given it all up for your mother and the family we could have been."

Rosa gaped as the man turned on his heel and strode from the Hampton House without a backward glance, tears burning behind her eyes as hurt, anger, and sorrow twisted in her heart.

Dan stared at Rosa seeing the pain in her eyes as tears began to fall. Instinctively he wrapped an arm around her pulling her close but her sharp intake of breath and whispered words had him springing back like a scalded cat.

"You!" Rosa hissed. "You are not a good man." She sprang to her feet glaring down at him then looking up as he stood.

"What? I'm trying to help." Dan matched her hard glare with his own, but flinched as she opened her mouth. He knew what was coming. Knew her accusations would cut to the bone but before she could speak a strong hand descended on his arm.

"You love birds come with me," Olive Hampton grasped them both by the wrist, her grip surprisingly strong for a woman her age. "We'll have a nice private chat in the parlor." Olive's voice sounded loud in the hushed dining hall but her determined tug had both parties rushing to keep up.

"Olive," Rosa protested.

"Not a word." Olive's tone was clipped and even Dan hesitated to speak before she told him to. "This is for your own good," the old woman said. "Now get in here and close the door."

Together the trio stepped into the living quarters of the Hampton family, the door snapping behind them with a click as Olive sagged into a chair.

"Olive are you unwell?" Rosa said, stooping to look at the older woman. "Should I get Daliah?" Worry creased Rosa's face and Dan's heart squeezed at her fear.

"No, no." Olive waved Rosa away. "Sit down. We need to talk." She waved her hand in front of her face for a moment closing her eyes as her breathing settled. "I'm getting too old for days like this."

"You are not so old," Rosa snapped, but her voice betrayed her convictions.

"I'm old enough to know trouble when I see it." Olive opened her eyes pointing to a simple settee across from her. "Sit down and tell me what that was all about. I thought you were going to kill that man." Olive looked between Dan and Rosa. "And you, what in the world were you doing announcing to the world that you and Rosa are getting married. "The whole town will know before dinner tonight."

"I was just trying to help," Dan protested. He sounded sullen even to his ears as emotions roiled through him like a stampeding herd.

"You may have helped the two of you straight to the altar."

"It will not come to that." Rosa flashed a hard look at Dan. "I will tell my father that we must wait. Eventually, he will go home. He cannot stay away forever."

Olive's harsh grunt made Rosa look back at her. "Dan would you be so kind as to put the kettle on in the kitchen for me? Rosa can make us some tea and explain who that man is exactly and why he thought he could come to Needful and take one of our own."

Rosa opened her mouth to protest then met Olive's eyes and nodded as Dan jumped to his feet and hobbled toward the other room without a backward glance.

"Tell me everything Rosa," Olive said weariness edging her voice. "There's more to this story than a wayward father coming to claim his child."

Chapter 15

Rosa walked into the kitchen and pulled down a teapot and a tin of black tea. Dan hadn't returned to the parlor but instead stood staring at the cookstove as if it might hold the secrets of the universe.

"Is that man really your father?" he asked as Rosa swilled the pot and added the tea.

"Yes." Rosa didn't meet Dan's eyes, but instead took three cups from a shelf and placed them on a tray then filled the pot with boiling water.

"Did you know he would come?"

"No!" Rosa turned a small creamer and sugar bowl in her hands. "I had hoped to never see him again in my life."

Dan nodded. "I'll do whatever I can to help," he offered lamely as Rosa added the teapot to the tray and hefted it in her hands. "Bring cookies," she spouted walking out of the kitchen and back into the parlor, her head held high.

Dan chuckled looking around him for something that might contain cookies and spying a cracker tin. Peeking inside he grinned at the array of crisp ginger snaps then hobbled after Rosa as fast as he could.

"Now," Olive was saying as Dan placed the tin on a small table. "Tell me everything Rosa and don't leave anything out."

Rosa lifted the teapot giving it a gentle swirl then pouring the amber brew into each cup.

"When I was a girl I loved my father," she began. "He would come to the house bringing us gifts and candy. It was like Christmas each time he came and my mother would light up with joy. She would press her best dress, fix her hair, and make sure that we all looked nice."

"Go on," Olive prompted taking a cookie and dunking it into her tea.

"Father would sweep in like a summer storm full of laughter and light. Often he would dance with my mother bringing her pretty dresses or other gifts. He always brought money, and when he would leave, Mother would take us to the market to buy something special. When we asked why our father did not live with us all of the time, she would only say that he had other responsibilities that kept him away, and she would grow sad. I did not understand for many years what she meant but eventually, as I grew older I learned."

Dan opened his mouth to ask a question but Olive's hard glared had him closing it on a cookie instead and he waited for Rosa to continue.

The woman beside him had such sorrow in her eyes as she spoke that he wanted to pull her tight, to hide her from all the bad things in the world, and never let them hurt her again.

"When I was eleven, my mother grew ill. She needed a doctor, and I went to the nearest town to find one. Always before I had gone to town with my mother and no one spoke more than a few words to us. They were eager to take our money, but they did not ask us in for tea or let their children play with us. I came to the town to fetch the doctor and as I walked, I noticed how the women looked at me. Several of them turned to whisper something to a friend, and soon I felt that they were all talking about me."

Olive nodded encouraging Rosa to go on though it was obvious that the telling was painful.

"When I found the doctor, there was another woman there. I did not know her, but she looked at me as if I was less than dirt. 'What do you want?' she asked her cold words hitting me like a physical blow. 'I have come for the doctor,' I told her. 'My mother is ill'."

Rosa looked up, her eyes full of tears. "She told me that she was not surprised that a woman like my mother would grow ill and that the world would be a better place without her in it. That any woman that would share her favors with a married man was evil and her children were nothing but..."

Dan reached out placing his hand over Rosa's knowing what she would say. "That's not right," he whispered. "It wasn't your fault. She shouldn't have spoken to you like that."

Rosa looked up, her eyes shining with tears, but she didn't jerk her hand away. "I ran," she said. "I ran all the way home and though I had not called the doctor, he still came. When Mother was better, I asked her if what the woman said was true. She did not deny it. She didn't even try to defend herself. She knew what she had done was wrong, but she would not give up this man."

"When did you meet Raul?" Olive asked gently. "When did you marry him?"

A wan smile spread across Rosa's face and she pulled her hand from Dan's brushing the tears from her eyes. "Raul was from the town. He would come with his father and work around our house. They were very poor, but they worked hard. Already his brother, Rivera was a bad one. He took things that did not belong to him. He was always fighting and causing trouble. Once he came to Mother and told her she had not paid enough for the work that his father had done, he demanded more and she gave it to him."

Olive pulled a handkerchief from her dress sleeve and handed it to Rosa. "Go on dear."

Rosa smiled as memories flooded her mind. "Raul was good. He would come to help, but not want any money. He fixed our chicken coop or cleaned the well. Always he was laughing telling jokes. He had honor even then." Rosa collapsed into tears sobbing with grief, loss, and frustration.

Olive nodded to Dan and he pulled Rosa to him wrapping her in his arms until she cried herself out.

"How old were you when you married Raul?" Olive finally asked as Rosa dried her eyes. "Why didn't your father know?"

"I ran away," Rosa said biting her lip to control her voice. "Raul told me he loved me, and that as soon as he had a place of his own he would marry me. I told him that I was, I was the daughter of an unwed mother, but he didn't care. He loved me and would give me the home I deserved. I didn't want to wait. I could feel the eyes of our town on me always and only wanted to escape. We ran away when I turned seventeen and were married at a small church. The rest you know."

Chapter 16

Dan clasped his hands in his lap forcing himself not to spring to his feet and pace the cozy room. He was angry at the unfairness of it all. Rosa had found love and a man who was good, honest, and true only to lose him in a horrible mistake. It wasn't her fault that life had been so unfair. She wasn't to blame for her parent's choices.

"Rosa," Ellen stepped into the room with Rosa's daughter Christina on her hip. "I think she wants you, she was fussy when she woke from her nap," the pretty blonde woman said putting the little girl down and aiming her toward her mother. "You all take your time," the other woman said with a grin. "We have everything under control."

Christina giggled, her bright smile twinkling in her eyes as she toddled across the room as Ellen turned around leaving them alone once more.

Rosa leaned forward extending her hands as her eyes brightened with joy at the sight of her daughter but her smile faltered as Christina made her way to Dan trying to climb into his lap.

Dan's eyes widened as the little girl tried to pull herself up and instinctively his hand reached under her arms lifting her onto his knees. The little girl wriggled onto his lap snuggling close to his chest and closing her eyes.

Olive's chuckle made both Dan and Rosa start and they turned to stare at the older woman. "Well at least she likes you," Olive laughed. "That should go a long way with convincing Mr. Hernandez that you really are going to marry Mayor Dan, Rosa."

"It will not come to that," Rosa said her lips forming a thin line as she looked back at her traitorous daughter. "He will go and things will return to normal."

Olive shook her head but didn't say anything else. "I'm going to my room," the old woman said. "You two had better get your stories straight if you plan on pulling this off. Your father may have made a few mistakes in his life, but he does not strike me as a fool."

Dan ran his hand over Christina's back, the motion soothing him as much as it did her. The little girl knew him well enough as he was often in town on business or at the Hampton House to share dinner with Spencer. Looking up, he met Rosa's dark eyes and she glared at him.

"Rosa," he tried but she turned away. "Rosa," he pressed. "It doesn't matter where you came from, or who your parents were. You're part of Needful and you're important to all of us." He felt his heart turn over with his last words. He had almost said she was important to him.

"You say this and yet you have done nothing but try to make me like my mother."

"No!" Dan yelped then settled as Christina started to sniffle. "No," he repeated softly his hands stroking Christina's back. "I never. I didn't. You miss understood."

Rosa raised a sculpted brow. "You say this, but how many times did you tell me you would give me a house, pay for my keep?"

"I meant that for just what it was." Dan handed Christina to her mother and stood, his ankle protesting. "Raul was my friend. He worked for me. I felt responsible. If I had known what he had done, I would have helped."

Rosa wrapped her daughter in her arms and gazed up at the Mayor of Needful. "Raul was not your responsibility. What he did was not your fault. He made a foolish decision and paid for it."

Dan turned, kneeling before the woman his eyes serious. "But you shouldn't have to pay for his mistake. That's why I wanted to help." His heart twisted as he gazed at her beautiful face, and he had to admit that he wanted Rosa. Was he any better than her father for his deception? "I'll do whatever it takes to give you the life you want Rosa.

You shouldn't have to worry about how you will provide for Christina. Let me help."

"I think I have no choice in the matter now," Rosa said meeting his eyes boldly. "You have told my father that you are marrying me. I hope he does not call your bluff."

Dan nodded slowly, silently hoping that the man did.

***

"Dan don't you think this is getting out of hand?" Spencer asked as he rode along with his brother a few days later. "Juan Xavier has hired William to ride to Dallas for supplies and some of his men left yesterday riding hard for the border with a list of things he wants from back home. He's already invested money into this wedding. You know, the wedding you and Rosa have no plans on following through with."

Dan pulled the bandana from his neck wiping his face and neck with it as his horse pranced nervously under him. "I know, I know," he grumbled. "But what am I supposed to do. If I tell the man, it's all a farce he'll drag Rosa and Christina back to Mexico with him."

"Not if she doesn't want to go," Spencer said his blue eyes taking on a steely glint. "I'm still the law here, and if a citizen of this town doesn't want to leave, I won't let anyone take them against their will."

"I know that," Dan agreed, re-tying the bandana and turning his horse back toward town. "But you just saw that Hernandez's men don't seem inclined to go anywhere without his say so, and that could cause a lot of trouble for Needful."

"So you're just going to go along with this even if it means you have to marry Rosa?"

Dan nodded feeling the heat rise up his neck and hoping his brother thought it was from the unseasonable weather. Summer was waning but the heat had returned full force over the little town.

Spencer tipped his head studying his younger brother from under the brim of his hat. He was starting to suspect that what Daliah had said was true and that Dan would willingly walk the aisle even for a chance at a fake marriage.

"Besides," Dan said as they ambled back toward town. "The worst thing that can happen is Brandon performs a fake wedding, and when Juan Xavier is gone, we'll just break it up again."

Spencer pulled in a deep breath of hot air letting it out slowly. "This has got to be about the dumbest idea you have ever had. All my life, I've been reminded that you're the sensible, level headed one, but I'm starting to suspect you've lost your mind."

Dan chuckled reaching over to pat his brother on the shoulder. They had just ridden out to check on the Hernandez camp where the idle cowboys had settled while they waited on their boss. "Don't worry Spence, if worse comes to worst you can always arrest me and throw me into jail for being a fool." Dan kicked his leggy roan into a gallop kicking up the dust in the road with a hearty laugh as Spencer raced to catch up.

Chapter 17

"Olive what am I supposed to do?" Rosa said as she stood on a stool letting Olive and the other Hampton women fit the fancy dress her father had sent for. It was long and a deep golden-white that shimmered in the sun pouring through the window of the parlor.

"We've been over this before," Olive said pulling at the waistline and pinning it to fit Rosa's slim waist. "You can either tell your father the truth, marry Dan, or go back to Mexico. Either way, we'll stand by you."

Rosa groaned then yelped as a pin pricked her. How had she gotten into this mess? Everything was out of control, but she didn't know how she would ever be able to stand up to her father. He was a man who was used to having his own way, and he had the money and the power to get it. She thought of Spencer's report of the hard men camped outside the town and didn't want to cause unrest in Needful.

Juan Xavier had always been an ambitious

man. He had married well merging his father's business interest with his father-in-law's ranch and horse breeding operation. No matter how much he did for her, no matter how much he told her that he had married her mother after his wife had died, she could not forgive him for his disregard for what was right, and the shame he had laid on his children.

"Arabela, would you see if you can find Mayor Dan?" Olive asked as she pushed the last pin into the dress and began to help Rosa out of the beautiful gown. "I think he and Rosa need to talk."

Rosa groaned stepping into her simple calico dress once more and letting Ellen button it up the back. She felt lost, adrift in a sea of confusion and doubt. Why couldn't her father just go home? Why couldn't he leave her alone with her daughter and friends?

"I'll fetch tea," Shililiah said with a grin, dragging her long copper-gold braid over one shoulder, her fingers lingering on the cool satin of the wedding dress. "I think you need it," she added patting Rosa on a shoulder as she slumped into a chair covering her eyes with her hand.

Rosa leaned her head back against the cushion of the chair listening to the bustle and rattle of the other women around her as they gathered up the gown, placed something on a table, and shuffled out leaving the room in silence.

"Dios Christos," Rosa whispered in her native tongue. "Show me the way."

***

Dan stepped into the room his eyes falling on Rosa and he drank her in. Her head was tipped back exposing the smooth line of her throat and he swallowed pushing thoughts of kissing her from his mind. The woman's eyes were closed and she looked weary, drained of the usual fire that seemed to burn at her core.

"Rosa," he whispered waiting for her to respond and smiling when she cracked one eye open to look at him.

"Go away," Rosa said closing her eye. "I want to be alone."

Dan chuckled pleased to see she was still able to snap at him. He knew that this charade was wearing her down. "I don't think so," his voice was warm and light, and his smile widened when she sat up to glare at him. "Olive sent for me and I'm not going back out there until she thinks I've done whatever it is she thinks I should do."

"Fine," Rosa said leaning forward and pouring herself a cup of tea from the pot that had been placed on the small table before her. "What do you want?"

You. The thought zipped through Dan's mind making him jump, but he covered his mistake by taking a chair and looking at the teapot.

Rosa sat her cup down pouring a second one and handing it to him. "I did not know you liked tea."

"I don't," Dan grinned. "But it gives me something to do."

Rosa's sharp bark of laughter settled his nerves and together they shared a moment of joy in the midst of chaos.

"Why are you here?" Rosa asked growing serious once more. "I thought a man was not supposed to see the bride before the wedding."

Dan chuckled, a sound between a bark and a groan. "That's just on the wedding day," he said. "Rosa whatever you want I'll do it." The cowboy's words tumbled over each other in a rush. "I don't care if we have to go through with this wedding to convince your father you'll be all right. I can always pay Brandon to do a fake wedding, and then once your father is gone you can come back to the Hampton House, or you can have that house I promised. You don't need to worry about anything ever again."

Rosa's laugh was bitter but she met his eyes. "I do not think that is how life works Mr. Gaines. There are always cares one way or another. I am too tired to fight my father anymore, and I do not want to drag this out anymore. If you will talk to the preacher I say we go through with the wedding, and when my father and his vaqueros leave, we will return to our own lives."

Dan nodded. "Don't you worry about a thing. This will all work out the way it should, you'll see." He reached across the table to place his hand on hers.

Rosa felt the warmth from Dan's hand travel up her arm and her heart softened toward the man. She was tired of fighting, tired of always being strong. His touch was gentle, demanding nothing of her, and she was grateful for the small connection. She only hoped that when the time came she could trust him to play his part and convince her father that they were truly wed. Hopefully, that would convince him and he would return to Mexico and leave her and Christina alone. Olive kept insisting he was honorable and would do the right thing. She hoped her friend was right.

"Thank you," she whispered returning Dan's squeeze. "Only a few more days and you will be free once more."

Dan nodded slowly studying Rosa's face. She looked sad and he wondered if she would miss him once this whole mess was over. It was going to be tough explaining the break up to his men as only Spencer and a few others knew that he and Rosa were not truly engaged. The town was gearing up for a big celebration and a chance to see their mayor married in style. There hadn't been this much excitement since the Fourth of July, and he couldn't ruin everyone's fun let alone risk the chance that Rosa's father would find out the whole thing was staged to get him to leave town.

"I guess I'll see you at the church on Sunday then," Dan said rising and releasing her hand reluctantly. "I'm sure you'll make a beautiful bride."

Rosa looked up surprised by Mayor Dan's words. They were kind and he seemed to have meant every one of them. Perhaps it was a fake wedding, but his words reminded her that she was a woman. Raul had often told her how beautiful and special she was, and it felt good to hear it again.

"I will do my best," she said lowering her eyes.

Dan slipped out the side door of the Hampton House leaving Rosa alone with her thoughts. Daliah had taken Christina while Olive and the other women helped with her fitting. Juan Xavier had ordered a large wedding dinner and invited the whole town to the festivities. This whole thing was completely out of control.

Perhaps it would be fun dressing the part of a bride and wearing a fancy gown. Rosa's wedding to Raul had been simple with no fan-fair or friends. They had said their 'I-dos' before the priest and started on their own, leaving behind everything they had ever known.

This wedding was not real, but instead of

a day that would change everything, it would allow things to stay the same. She and Christina would be allowed to stay in Needful surrounded by people she loved. Friends who were more like family. It wasn't easy being a mother alone in the world, but here at the Hampton House and in Needful as a whole she felt that she belonged.

For a moment, her mind flashed back to a time not long ago when her wicked brother-in-law had kidnapped her and Ruth. The men of the town had ridden to their rescue without a second thought, not resting until they had brought them both safely home and seen justice done for the Rivera gang.

Rosa brushed her fingers over her lips remembered Dan Gaines and his response to finding her. He had swept her into his arms, lifting her off the ground and kissed her as a feeling of joy and relief washed over her.

Rosa grinned remembering how she had pulled her hand free cuffing the man so hard he had nearly dropped her. Something inside pinched and she felt a moment of guilt for her behavior. Perhaps he had simply been overcome with relief at finding them. Her lips tingled with remembrance of the moment and a warm ripple that had nothing to do with anger rolled down her spine.

Rosa sat up straighter, her eyes going wide as her fingers lingered on her lips. If she married Daniel Gaines would he kiss her in the church for all to see?

***

Rosa felt herself tremble as Olive laced up her corset tying it tight as Arabela and Shi lifted the elegant gown preparing to slip it over her head. Rosa closed her eyes trying to choke back the fear and nervousness that assaulted her senses.

"You stop that," Olive growled into her ear. "Dan isn't going to mistreat you or take advantage. He's a good man even if you don't know it. Have I steered you wrong yet?"

"No," Rosa's voice was a tiny squeak, and she let the tension slip from her shoulders. If anything went wrong, she knew that Olive and Orville, the whole family really, would take her back and protect her. It was just so hard to trust.

"You're going to your wedding, not the gallows," Olive continued and Rosa felt her lips twitch as the Hampton women slipped the golden gown over her head. It was a beautiful dress, and she still couldn't believe that she was wearing such a thing.

The satin rippled like water in a long cascade down her back, the train widening slightly from the skirt that fell to just above her slippered feet. Gold embossed stitching picked out the dropped waist and etched the scooped neckline, and she tugged at it trying to cover the glimpse of cleavage it revealed.

"It is too low," she said her eyes following the row of pearl buttons that ended at the point of the dropped waist.

"It is not," Olive laughed. "Now stop fidgeting and let us get you ready. You look beautiful."

Rosa looked up into Olive's dark eyes shocked at the woman's words. "Me?"

"Yes you," Olive said her eyes softening as she smiled. "You are a beautiful woman Rosa you should enjoy this day. Even if you and Dan don't stay married, you can enjoy the day. Let us make a fuss over you. Make your father believe that you are happy and loved."

"Well you are," Ellen spoke up. Ellen was the quietest of the three Hampton daughters-in-law. "We love you," she finished with a smile.

Rosa felt her throat close with emotion and a bright tear trembled on her cheek. "I don't know what to say."

"You don't need to say anything," Arabela looked down at her. The woman was tall, stately, and her raven black hair glistened in the light that shone through the window. "We are your friends, your family. Make today wonderful." A rare smile graced the woman's face and Rosa sighed.

"I will do my best," Rosa agreed.

"And don't let that temper of yours get the better of you either," Shililiah grinned. "I know men can be infuriating sometimes, but today you need to get along and make everyone believe that Dan is your dream come true. You can fight with him later," she added with a laugh.

The tension that had hung in the room seemed to snap and Rosa's laugh mingled with the others.

"Besides," Arabela added, one brow raised in a haughty glance. "You don't want to have a real fight until you know you can enjoy the making up."

Rosa covered her mouth surprised at the other woman's words but nodded. There was so much more to the dark-haired woman than most people realized. Arabela seemed aloof, unapproachable even. Rosa hoped that over time they might truly become friends. Had it only been this winter that the Hampton boys had arrived in Needful with their families?

Olive placed a veil on Rosa's head attaching it carefully to her hair with ivory combs. Shi had done something to Rosa's lush locks earlier, and she was careful not to move while Olive secured the veil for fear of making a mess of the whole thing.

"There, now you can look." Olive pulled the

cover off of a long mirror and Rosa gaped. She looked like some sort of Spanish princess with the high crown of satin roses that held the long veil on her head.

"Is that really me?" Rosa shifted forward in a rustle of satin pulling the long straight sleeves forward so that the gold stitching on the cuff touched her hand.

None of it seemed real. It was as if Rosa were walking through a dream or living in a fairytale. A smile spread across her face and she lifted her chin regally. She would take Olive's advice. She would embrace the day and live one moment as a princess from a storybook.

"I am ready," she said twisting her body and letting the dress twirl around her in an ocean of satin and lace. "Let us go."

Chapter 18

"Stop fidgeting," Spencer said as he straightened his brother's string tie. "You'd think this was a real wedding the way you. I wasn't this nervous when I married Daliah."

Dan chuckled remembering his brother's wedding. A day he had never believed he would see again.

"What ya nervous for Uncle Dan," Chad asked smoothing his dress jacket with pride. "Pa married Daliah and look at how good that went. What could go wrong with you marryin' Rosa? You even get a daughter in the mix just like Daliah got me."

Dan grinned at his nephew brushing the boy's pale hair from his eyes. "Let's just say I didn't expect this to happen this way."

"I like Rosa," Chad continued. "Daliah says she has a good heart and a lot of love to share."

Dan raised his brows looking at his brother who only shrugged. "Daliah has her own notions about this whole thing."

Dan squinted knowing there was more his brother hadn't said. "I don't suppose you'd like to enlighten me?"

"No," Spencer grinned, casting a glance at his son. "You'll figure it out on your own."

Chad rolled his eyes. "Grown-ups are confusing," he grumbled turning to peek out the door of the small parsonage. "They're coming." The boy said bouncing with excitement. "I can see Daliah with Christina and they have a basket of flowers."

Dan swallowed hard calling himself every kind of fool for going through with this. He kept telling himself he was looking out for Rosa. Raul would want to know she was safe and taken care of, but other thoughts kept zooming to the surface of his brain.

Over the past week, he had spent a good deal of time with Juan Xavier, and the man had grilled him extensively about his ranch, his job as mayor, and his character as a whole. He had done his best to be respectful and to convince the man that this was a real marriage.

He and Rosa had determined that they should keep things simple and had informed her father that they had only realized when Dan rescued her that there was anything between them. So far, the ruse seemed to be working, and he hoped they could get through the ceremony without fighting.

"Time to go, little brother," Spencer said slapping him on the shoulder and hurrying him around to the back door of the church.

In a matter of moments, Dan was standing at the front of the church the eyes of the town's people gazing on him approvingly as he awaited his fate.

***

Rosa took her father's arm as Ellen smoothed her train behind her.

"You look so like your mother," Juan Xavier said his dark eyes filling with regret.

Rosa stared at the man she barely knew for a long moment then nodded once. "I believe we have a wedding to attend."

The doors before them opened, Jubal and Joseph Hampton beaming at them from each side of the aisle. "It's about time," they whispered and Rosa shifted nervously on her father's arm.

"Christina," Rosa whispered watching as Daliah led her toddler down the aisle tossing flowers on the floor with abandon. Rosa's heart swelled, and a spark of joy lit in her soul. Her daughter would never know the pain and shame that Rosa had. She was free of the darkness that had plagued her life.

Taking a deep breath Rosa lifted her chin then paused as her eyes met the simmering blue of Dan's.

A bright smile flickered over her face as she smoother her skirt while the man gaped. He looked like a fish out of water, and she wanted to place her finger under his chin to snap his mouth shut.

Squeezing her father's arm Rosa poured all the joy, hope, and cheer she could find into her smile. She would convince her father that she was ready to become the loving and adoring wife of the man who stood at the front of the church. She could do this. She could make him believe then go back to the way things were.

***

Dan felt his jaw go slack and he stood gaping at the vision that had entered the church. Rosa, dressed in some shimmering gown stepped into the aisle like a queen walking to her throne. Her face glowed with joy and love and his heart jumped at the sight of her. She was breathtaking, and he couldn't breathe as her radiant eyes met his.

The look she bestowed upon him filled him with light, and he knew he was lost. There was no coming back from this. He knew, as surely as there was a sun in the sky, that he loved Rosa Rodriguez. He couldn't pinpoint the moment it had happened, but he knew that no matter what he told himself the truth was there. He, Dan Gaines, was in love with Rosa.

Rosa's hand came to rest on Dan's and he turned snapping his mouth shut as his eyes studied her face. In all the history of weddings, he was sure that there had never been a more beautiful bride, and his heart tugged toward her.

The preacher was saying something and Juan Xavier replied releasing Rosa's hand and stepping back leaving the two of them alone.

"You look beautiful," Dan whispered but Brandon cleared his throat drawing his attention.

"Dearly Beloved," the spindly preacher with a mop of dark curls on his head intoned but Dan barely heard the words. His eyes kept flicking back to Rosa and the bright smile and shining eyes she bestowed upon him. It was like a dream. A perfect wonderland, where he would be her husband, and they could spend their lives filling each day with love.

"Dan," Brandon said bumping Dan's elbow. "You need to repeat the words." He nodded toward Spencer who was holding out a small gold band and Dan flushed.

Taking the ring from his brother, Dan set it at the tip of Rosa's delicate finger and repeated the words the preacher gave him. His eyes were locked on Rosa's, and he saw something flicker in their depths. Laughter? Hope? Love? He wasn't sure what it was, but as he said his vows each one became very real and something solid seemed to settle in his soul. He would protect, care for, and provide for Rosa. He would keep her safe and happy even if that meant turning away from her and letting her have the life she wanted without him.

As Rosa began to speak Dan's eyes flickered toward Juan Xavier who beamed with joy and delight. At least they had fooled her father and soon Rosa could find her peace once more.

Rosa's voice was a breathy whisper as she spoke the words of devotion, obedience, and love before the entire town and Dan turned his eyes back to her encouraging her with his thoughts. *I promise you'll be safe.* He thought. *I promise you'll be provided for. I promise you'll be loved.*

A moment later and he was being instructed to kiss his bride. His lips fell on Rosa's as he put every hope, desire, and promise into that gentle brush of lips.

***

After the wedding, the party seemed to go on forever, and Dan was exhausted with well-wishers, dancing, and food. He was looking forward to taking Rosa and Christina home to the ranch and settling them in the rooms he had prepared. He hoped that Juan Xavier would leave sooner rather than later now that his daughter was wed. He wasn't sure how long he would be able to live with the woman without making a fool of himself.

The old cook, his ranch hands, and the house help would be a buffer between them and would hopefully make life more bearable once they made it home.

"You make a very handsome couple," Juan Xavier smiled stepping up to Dan and patting him on his shoulder. Rosa was making the rounds talking and chatting with the women of Needful, her cheeks rosy with exertion and excitement. It was an amazing party and behind them a group of men started playing another slow song.

"I have one more gift for you today," the shorter man said. "There were many things I never was able to do for the woman I loved," he said his eyes full of deep sorrow. "I am not proud of what I did," he continued. "I have made many mistakes, but I am trying to make up for that now. I seek," he paused looking for the right word. "Absolution."

Dan nodded taking the man at his word. It was obvious that he regretted the lost relationship with his daughter and readily admitted that he had not lived his life in the best way.

"Juan Xavier," Dan started. "You don't need to do anything else for us. You know I'll take care of your daughter."

For a long moment, the older man said nothing as he studied Dan's face. "I believe this," he said.

"This I do not doubt. I know that you will do everything possible to make my daughter happy and to provide for her, but do not be fooled. As her mother, I know that sometimes Rosa does not know what is best for her." Juan Xavier chuckled, startling Dan, but then he continued. "You are good for her but she is stubborn, independent, and full of fire. Do not give in to her if you love her. Be her match."

Dan blinked shocked at the man's words but was startled when his father-in-law pressed something into Dan's hands. "Your honeymoon," Juan Xavier tipped his head spinning on his heels and striding away.

Dan looked down at the small packet in his hands and his blood turned cold.

"Dan, are you feeling all right," Daliah and Spencer stepped up before him. "You look pale."

Dan peeled back the flap on the envelope and pulled out the steamboat tickets neatly written out in his name. Juan Xavier's final gift might very well be the death of him. He would never be able to survive a week in the same room with Rosa without losing his mind.

Daliah pulled the papers from his hands scanning them and letting out a little gasp. "This was not a part of the plan," she whispered handing the packet to Spencer. "What will you do?"

"Daliah?" Rosa whirled up to them dancing

Christina on her hip. "Is something wrong?"

Daliah turned meeting Rosa's dark eyes. "You're father," she said licking her lips nervously. "He left you a final gift."

Rosa looked between Daliah and Dan a feeling of dread filling her heart.

"He planned our honeymoon," Dan whispered all the blood draining from his face.

"What?" Rosa looked at the papers Spencer handed her and gasped. "We won't go."

"If we don't he'll never leave," Dan said knowing it was true. Juan Xavier had a ready crew of trusted men who would tend to his business interest in Mexico. He could be gone from home for a long time if he chose to.

"I won't." Rosa's statement was emphatic.

Dan closed his eyes turning to look at her. "I don't think we have a choice."

"But what about Christina?" she bulked. "I cannot just leave my daughter."

Christina reached for Daliah with a giggle and the other woman took her in her arms. "How long is the trip?" the town healer asked.

"Four days," Dan said peering at the pages over Rosa's shoulder once more.

"Ah, there you are," Juan Xavier called hurrying to them and wrapping an arm around both of them. "You are happy yes? It is my gift to you. Your mother always wanted to go on a paddlewheel boat. I did this to honor her."

Rosa tried to force a smile, but it felt odd on her face. "I don't think we can just leave," she tried. "I have Christina, Dan has responsibilities."

"You have friends here; this town will not blow away on the wind if you take a few days to be alone."

Rosa looked between her father and the man she had just wed, fear clutching at her heart as she noted the glint of suspicion in Juan Xavier's eye.

"Perhaps we could go later," Rosa suggested. "After we are settled."

"Is there some problem?" Her father's voice turned harsh as his expression darkened. "Will you not take this gift from me? You need to be alone so that you will know who you will be together."

"We'll go," Dan replied quickly wrapping an arm around Rosa and pulling her close. "I'm sure Spencer and Daliah will be able to look after Needful and Christina for a day or two."

Rosa tipped her head up looking at the man, her eyes hard. Closing her eyes for a moment Rosa forced her temper back down. She trusted Daliah and the Hamptons to look after her daughter, but could she trust herself alone with Daniel Gaines.

So far, he had kept his word at every turn, but this would be much more difficult.

Opening her eyes she plastered a smile to her face and sighed up at Dan. "It will be a lovely rest," she said hoping he would understand her meaning. "Thank you, father."

Chapter 19

Juan Xavier waved to his daughter as she stood at the rail of the large white boat that would ferry her along the dark waters of the big river. He had given her this gift, this chance to have time to be a good wife to her new husband. He had missed so much of her life after she had married Raul, and he couldn't blame her for not wanting anything to do with him. He knew his sins were many, but he was trying to set things right.

Rosa had felt the shame of her childhood more keenly than any of the others. His sons had come to him to work at the ranch as soon as they were old enough, and the knowledge that they were his flesh and blood had been enough to silence the harsh whispers of society.

Rosa however had not been privy to that kind of protection. She had discovered the truth as a girl and had carried his guilt with her for far too long. When she had married Raul and left to start a life on her own, he had been happy for her though a tiny piece of his heart had gone. Now he had a chance to start over just like Rosa.

When his first wife had died he had wanted to marry his true love immediately, but she had waited. Waited until her other children were old enough to understand and accept the truth. When they were wed, his family had finally become legitimate taking his name for the first time and finding their place in society anew. His life with Rosa's mother had been too short, and now he had only her three brothers and younger sister to love.

He lifted his hand again as he smiled at his daughter confident that now he could go home. In time he would come again and perhaps what he had done for Rosa would soften her heart toward him. For now, he would entrust her to the loving arms of her new husband. Dan was a good man, better than he had ever been, and he loved Rosa.

"We ride," he called turning back to his men who had accompanied the couple to the river to see them safely aboard. "Rosa will be happy. We go home."

The men cheered and turned their horses toward home following him back to their land.

***

"Are you sure we can't get off at the first stop and take the stage home?" Rosa asked as she watched her father and his men ride away. "We could be back in Needful tomorrow and you could go home."

"Rosa," Dan said patiently, taking her hand and placing it on his arm. "We'll only be gone a few days. Why don't you try to enjoy the trip? I've never been on a steamboat before, it could be interesting."

Rosa sagged in defeat. She had known he would say something reasonable like that, but she hated being away from Christina. Besides, she wanted this pretend marriage to end sooner rather than later. She was getting entirely too comfortable with the rancher.

"You don't think father will come back do you?" she asked her eyes wide with fright.

"Not for a while anyway," Dan said. "We'll worry about that when the time comes." For a moment, his eyes grew serious, and he wanted to pour out all the thoughts that kept racing through his head. He wanted to tell her that everything would be all right and that he would love and protect her forever if she would only allow it. Instead, he grinned wickedly and turned her down the wide expanse of the deck. "Let's find the dining hall," he laughed. "It's time you let someone else cook for you."

Rosa looked up at Dan surprised by his glee and smiled. It might be nice to let someone else spoil her for a bit. "Do you think the food will be good?"

"I'm not fussy," Dan laughed, "but I'd bet it's got to be or people wouldn't pay to eat it."

Rosa smiled feeling a weight slip from her shoulders at Dan's jovial tone. Perhaps she would be able to get through this trip without losing her mind. She would do her best to enjoy this honeymoon even if she did not love the man she was with. She studied his handsome face wondering if she ever could.

An older couple strolled by taking the evening air and Rosa wondered what they saw when they looked at her. Her dark eyes turned to Dan studying him. He was a handsome man, though rather thin in her opinion. He was still smiling and it did something to his face. Gone was the serious, insistent man from Needful, replaced by someone who seemed to be enjoying these moments with her.

"Something smells good," Rosa mused as they approached a brightly lit narrow room on the top deck. "I think we are in time for dinner."

Dan pulled his tickets from the pocket of his coat showing them to a waiter who seated them at a long table full of other passengers. He gazed around curiously taking note of the surrounding people. Several older couples sat together chatting or sipping wine. He was glad he had decided to wear his suit for the trip but tugged at the collar of his shirt trying to ease the pull of his tie.

A few families sat along one side of the table and two dark men watched the guests from each corner of the dining table.

Dan helped Rosa to a seat feeling the eyes of the men fall on his lovely pseudo-wife. She was more beautiful than she knew, and he wasn't surprised at the attention she received.

Dan slipped into the seat next to Rosa scooting it a little closer and leaning into her as if to tell her a joke.

"I don't like the looks of those two men on either end of the table." Dan was careful to keep the smile on his face. "Please watch yourself if you go out on your own. Now smile as if I said something funny."

Rosa tittered softly turning to look at Dan as her eyes flicked down the table. The man in the black frock coat did look rather sinister with a small black beard and a thin mustache.

Rosa leaned into Dan and the heady aroma of her perfume swamped his brain as she whispered in his ear. "They do not look trustworthy."

"Oh look, Harold," a buxom woman in a gaudy dress said. "We have newlyweds onboard." The woman's gray eyes twinkled with delight as she wiggled her fingers in the direction of Dan and Rosa. "I'm right aren't I?" she beamed.

Dan draped his arm around Rosa giving everyone a delighted grin. "You have a good eye," he grinned. "How did you know?"

"It's all the whispering." The portly man at the woman's side huffed. "When you've been married as long as we have, you see things," he added touching a finger to his nose. "I'm Harold Fritz," he offered, jabbing a thumb in his direction, and this is my wife "Matilda. Say hello Matilda."

"Hello," the woman offered with a wink and a grin as she toyed with the string of pearls around her neck. "I hope you have a lovely time. Steamboats are so relaxing."

From the corner of his eye, Dan saw one of the men rise, excusing himself politely as he pulled a long slim cheroot from his pocket and stepped out the door. There was something not quite right about him or the other one who was focused on his food. They would bear watching, and he would keep Rosa close just to be safe.

Chapter 20

Dan led Rosa to their room after dinner his nerves jangling at every sound. He had never traveled by steamboat before and had no idea what to expect. Perhaps they would have two small beds and a changing screen so that he could afford Rosa her privacy. He tugged at his collar again as the night grew suddenly warm.

Rosa opened the door and stopped staring at the large bed fastened on one side to the wall. There was a small clothing press and a washstand set in a small stand that was firmly attached to the deck. Someone had delivered their bags and had lit a lamp, from which the flickering flame cast the room into a warm glow.

"You must ask for another room," Rosa said wheeling to glare at him as if he had made these arrangements himself. "There is only one bed."

"I can see that," Dan whispered pulling her into the room and closing the door. "I don't think we can change rooms now that we're on the water though."

Rosa glared at him. "I am not sleeping in that bed with you," she flared an odd shiver running down her spine. "We agreed that this is a fake marriage and that once my father was gone, we could end it. I will be ashamed if I share a bed with you."

"Rosa," Dan reached out trying to take her by the arms, but she jerked back her dark eyes murderous. "Rosa," Dan repeated lifting his hands in surrender. "No one is going to know if we shared a bed or not." He felt his face flush red at Rosa's sharp intake of breath. "No, no! That's not what I meant. I'm trying to say. I'll sleep on the floor, and you can have the bed. When we get back to Needful, we'll just say we had separate beds or something."

Rosa eyed Dan suspiciously. Would he truly be willing to sleep on the floor of a rolling ship while she took what looked like a very comfortable bed? She closed her eyes trying to keep her thoughts calm. So far he had kept his word on every single thing he had promised. Even if he hadn't, she only had herself to blame. She had agreed to this mad idea, and now here she was stuck in a room with the one man she had tried to avoid at all costs.

"Very well," she said, "but you must go outside while I change."

Dan chuckled but didn't say a word, stepping back out onto the deck and walking to the rail. The night air brushed against his skin and he closed his eyes drinking in the smells of water and green things along the shore. Bright stars sparkled like diamonds in the sky, and he wished he could pull one down and give it to Rosa. He still couldn't get his head around what had happened, but somewhere between trying to convince her that he owed her a living and the moments his lips had brushed hers in the little church of Needful, he had surrendered to the feelings in his heart.

The door to his room opened a crack and Rosa peeked around the edge. "You can come in now," she whispered looking both directions then rushing away in a shuffle of bare feet.

Dan grabbed the door as it was swinging wide and caught just a glimpse of Rosa gathering her long nightgown around shapely ankles as she leapt into the double bed. In a moment she had the blankets pulled to her chin, but the sight of those ankles was sure to keep him up half the night.

"Do I at least get a pillow?" Dan grumbled feeling as grouchy as a doused cat.

Rosa pointed a finger toward the far wall and he shook his head at the pillow and blankets laid out for him. He was on his honeymoon and sleeping on the floor. Only he could end up married to the woman he loved, only to find himself sleeping on the cold hard floor on their wedding night.

Kicking off his boots and hanging his coat over a chair he slipped between the blankets with a groan of self-loathing.

"Goodnight," he mumbled reaching up and turning down the wick of the oil lamp.

"Goodnight." Rosa's single word hung in the darkness between them a shroud of longing and despair. It was going to be a long night.

Chapter 21

Rosa woke in a strange room the darkness around her pressing on her like a living thing. With a start, she sat up in bed her mind frantically trying to determine where she was, as her heart beat out a frantic pace.

A soft snore from one corner of the room made Rosa turn squinting into the darkness as everything came rushing back. She was on a boat with Dan Gaines pretending to be his wife. Settling back into the bed she felt the steady thrum of the paddlewheel engines through the mattress, the slosh of water far below barely audible in the quiet of the night, and Rosa desperately wanted to go home.

A warm tear trickled from her eye as she longed to watch her daughter sleep. Deep loneliness filled Rosa, and once again, she found herself wondering why Raul could not have stayed with her. Why he couldn't have been content to manage on the little they had. A soft shuffling noise nearby made Rosa turn toward the sound and she could just make out the outline of Mr. Gaines where he curled in the blankets.

Doubts assailed her as she stared at the slightly darker space that marked the rancher's lithe body. She was surprised he hadn't put up more of a fight about sleeping on the floor and the memory tugged her lips into a smile. Perhaps the Mayor of Needful was what he appeared, and he truly wanted nothing from her.

When he had first draped his arm around her, confronting her father with the news that they were engaged, she was sure he was trying once more to get her to agree to be his woman, but he had actually gone through with the wedding, and now here he was sleeping on the floor of their small stateroom.

"What do you want?" Rosa whispered covering her mouth with a hand when the cowboy stirred. Everyone wanted something in this world. Nothing was free. With a heavy sigh, she pulled the blankets back over her shoulders, warding off the chill of the night. Tomorrow she would do her best to enjoy the journey. She had never had such an adventure before, and she didn't want to let it slip through her fingers like sand. When she returned to Needful, life would go back to normal, just the way she liked it.

***

Dan shifted on the hard floor feeling the slight roll of the ship beneath him as the hard boards made his shoulder ache. He had heard Rosa's gasp and seen her sit up in bed and his whole body had tensed. Had she heard something? Was someone outside their room? Only silence met his ears as he waited and watched.

After several long seconds, Rosa flopped back into the bed and he stifled a groan at the thought of the soft mattress. He was sure Rosa must be missing Christina and would be thankful when this trip was over. He didn't want to see the longing in her eyes each time she thought about her little girl.

A whisper drifted toward him as the woman rolled to her side facing him and he bit back his immediate reply to the question that hung in the room. *You,* his mind screamed as he released his heart completely. He might never have Rosa's love, but he could be sure to have her wellbeing at heart. No matter what it took he would ensure she never went without as long as she lived in Needful.

***

Morning broke cool and bright and Rosa sat up stretching sleepily. Once her mind had settled, she had slept well, lulled by the gentle cadence of the steamboat.

"You must go," she said turning to look at Dan who was rubbing the sleep from his eyes. He didn't look like he had slept well, and the harsh rasp of whiskers under his hand made her smile.

"Go where?" Dan asked a yawn cracking his jaw.

"Out." Rosa's word was flat. "I wish to dress."

Dan nodded pushing himself to his feet with a low groan and rolling his shoulder to try to work out some of the stiffness. A moment later he had stomped into his boots, grabbed his hat, and was standing alone by the railing.

"Well good morning," the older woman from dinner the night before grinned. "Waiting on your wife?" Her bright smile and devilish twinkle made Dan grin.

"Yes," he admitted. "She's changing."

"Still shy in front of you?" Matilda's question was more a statement and Dan didn't bother to reply. "She'll get over that in time," the woman laughed. "One of these days." She added patting his arm. "How long have you been married?"

"Since yesterday morning." Dan's face fell as he thought about the fact that he would have to let Rosa go when they returned home.

"Don't look so glum. You'll adjust." Matilda grinned. "It can be a little rocky in the beginning as you get to know each other better. No matter how much you think you know someone before you marry, living with them can be a bit of a revelation. I can see you love her very much."

Dan turned back to the rail trying to hide the

frustration on his face.

"Oh, it's like that."

"Like what?" Dan turned half in irritation, half in shock

"There are those that say in a relationship one will always love better than the other but that my dear boy is poppycock. Throughout marriage sometimes one has to love the other a bit more and in turn be loved more when they are not so loveable." The older woman giggled shaking her head. "I don't think that made any sense, but it will. If you love that girl, just keep loving her, and in time, she'll give you her whole heart. In the end, it doesn't matter anyway because I can see you're smitten no matter what."

Dan turned, studying the woman for a moment then nodded. "Thanks," he said.

"You're welcome," she laughed. "Now I believe it is time for breakfast." Matilda turned with a titter, gliding away like a ship at sail.

Chapter 22

Dan offered Rosa his arm as he closed the door to their room and headed down the covered deck toward the dining area. She looked lovely in a dark green dress with wide skirts and a heavy ruffle that sloped from the bustle at the back.

"You look nice," Dan said before his mind could catch up with his mouth.

"Father insisted on several new dresses." Rosa shook her head in disgust. "I do not know why he spent this money. I will not need a dress like this for cooking at the Hampton House."

"Enjoy it while you can." Dan looked down on his diminutive fake wife. "You might as well have fun while you can." He spoke his words out loud but knew that they were as much for him as they were for Rosa.

Rosa tipped her head toward him a playful smile spring to her lips. "This is good advice," she laughed. "Today I am playing house as I did as a child only this time I will not have to make mud pies for dinner."

Dan laughed the sound echoing out across the water and bouncing back at them like a boomerang. "I'm very grateful for that."

"You never know," Rosa grinned. "You might like my mud pies. I am told I make very good ones."

Dan's laughter ushered them into the long thin dining area, and he dropped his hand to the small of Rosa's back guiding her to a chair near Harold and Matilda. His eyes fell on one of the hard-looking men sitting at the end of the table giving the man a curt nod.

Helping Rosa into her chair Dan greeted their companions then started filling a plate with bacon, eggs, and ham. Within moments Rosa was engaged in conversation with the older woman. This whole thing did feel like pretend as Rosa had said, and Dan grinned, thinking that in a fairytale the hero would not end up sleeping on the floor instead of in a nice soft bed with his beautiful new bride.

The man Dan knew as Harold poured a cup of coffee handing it to Dan with a wink. "You look like you could use it," he whispered leaning across the table until his broad girth and brocade vest brushed his plate.

Dan blushed taking the coffee but managed a thank you. He flashed a glance at Rosa who was still chatting with the other man's wife. "What is there to do onboard today?" the cowboy asked as they both began eating.

"They have a few games on the upper deck," Harold said. "We like to take a stroll before lunch. Of course, you can sit on the deck and read a book if the weather holds."

Dan nodded thinking of how he might make Rosa's day brighter by choosing some activities she might enjoy.

A chair scraped at the end of the table and the lean man in the dark suit slipped out the door letting in a soft gust of cool air.

Rosa shivered as the breeze rolled over her. "I forgot my shawl," she said rising to her feet. "I will fetch it."

Dan stood trying to stop her but she waggled a finger in his face. "You eat your breakfast. I will only be a minute."

Dan opened his mouth to protest, but her hard glare snapped it shut once more. A light chuckle met his ears, and he turned to see Harold grinning at him with delight.

"I can see you have your hands full with that one," the older man said. "I'm sure she will be fine. What can happen in the time it takes to return to your room? Enjoy your breakfast."

Dan turned toward the door again his mind full of doubts, but he let himself slip back into his chair. If she wasn't back in a minute or two he would go after her. He had promised to keep her safe and not only for her father's sake.

Dan chatted politely with his dining companions but grew steadily uncomfortable as the minutes dragged and Rosa still didn't return. Finally giving in to his nerves, he stood excusing himself and headed for the door.

***

Rosa wrapped her arms around herself as the wind quickened bringing with it a decided chill. If she hadn't been so stubborn she would have let Dan go for her wrap instead of stepping outside into the cold. She had almost made it to her room when a dark shadow slipped from a door tucking a string of bright pearls in a coat pocket as he stepped to the next room.

Rosa scowled as she watched the man slip into her room and her temper rose, chasing away the misty chill of the morning.

"What are you doing?" she barked stepping through the still-open door. "This isn't your room."

Like lightning, the man struck grabbing Rosa's arm and twisting her toward him wrapping a hand over her mouth.

"You should not have returned, little bird," the man hissed in her ear, his voice sending a shiver down Rosa's spine. "Now your husband will be alone again."

Rosa kicked her feet trying to fight the man off but he hefted her from the floor by the waist while another man slipped through the door.

"What happened?" The second man spoke peering out the door. "How could you be so careless?"

"I didn't see her. One second she was at the table, the next she was here."

"She'll ruin everything."

"Not if we get rid of her," the sound of the man's voice made Rosa freeze with fear.

She shook her head her eyes going wide with fright, but she couldn't speak past her captor's hand.

"What do you mean?" the second man's eyes sparked like flint.

"An accident. It will be a shame that such a pretty woman fell over the rail." He leaned in brushing her cheek with his lips as a vulpine grin full of teeth overcame his face.

The second man grinned leaning out the door to be sure that they were alone. "Coast is clear," he snarled opening the door and grabbing Rosa's kicking feet, crushing her ankles in strong hands.

Rosa couldn't breathe. Visions of her life, her

daughter, her hopes flashed through her mind as the two men hauled her toward the railing. They were on the second-floor deck and the black water gleamed wickedly far below. If they tossed her over she would never survive. At best she would break her neck on impact, at worst she would drown, pulled to the murky depths of the great river.

A door down the hall slammed open and Rosa saw Dan racing toward her a murderous look on his face. Her eyes widened, heart soaring with hope as the hard metal railing bit into her hip. "Dan!" She screamed as her captor's grip loosened, but the word changed to a scream as she sailed overboard plunging toward the water below.

Chapter 23

Dan saw everything happen as he barreled down the deck at top speed, realizing with a sickening dread that he wouldn't be there fast enough. His heart stuttered as the two men he had watched suspiciously, lifted a struggling Rosa over the rail, releasing her and wheeled toward him.

As Rosa's scream split the air a glint of silver appeared in the taller man's hand and they both turned to face a charging Dan.

The world went red as Dan's bare fist connected with the smaller man's jaw and the deviant dropped to the deck, a burning pain ripped across Dan's ribs as he twisted away from the dazzling blade and rammed his elbow into the other man's outstretched arm. The knife rattled to the deck and Dan spun the man around grasping the back of his neck and bouncing his head off the railing.

The tall man in the dark coat slumped to the floor, half sprawled across his unconscious partner and Dan didn't even blink as he hurtled the railing and dropped, boots first, toward the churning water below.

***

The dark waters closed over Rosa's head as she plunged into the river the churning water from the forward momentum of the boat swirling her dangerously near the hull. She struggled, clawing for the surface as her heavy skirts, and thick crinolines pulled at her, dragging her toward the depths like some dark mythical creature of old.

Panic clutched her throat and Rosa kicked spinning once more as she pushed painfully toward fresh air. Something solid collided with her head and her mind went black like the waters around her and she knew no more.

Her life drifted before her like a slowly moving stream washing away the shame and regret of days gone by. She had found love and lost it. She had given life to a precious child who would grow up forgetting her as the years wore on. At that moment Rosa gave up. She released all the hurt, anger, and fear she had been holding in her heart and prayed that somehow she would make it home to see her baby just one more time. A vision of Dan flickered then faded into black.

***

Dan splashed into the water startled by the chill that engulfed him, then gave a mighty kick and stroked toward the light above him. He had to find Rosa. Gasping he sucked in a breath of air gazing around him for a glimmer of green, any indication of where Rosa was. The eddy along the edge of the boat swirled lifting something from the current and he plunged beneath the waves once more, searching, seeking, grasping.

God help me! He screamed silently as he searched the murky waters until his lungs burned and black spots danced before his eyes. Shooting to the surface, he gasped for breath, turning as he tread water looking for Rosa.

Another flutter near an old snag had him shooting downstream as the big orange paddles churned the water into foam. Dan's heart froze as fear clutched at him with icy claws. If Rosa had drifted under those wheels; no, he wouldn't think like that. Swimming hard, his long strokes brought him to the old log, it's battered and broken limbs skeletal in their bareness, he saw her. Rosa bobbed upward her heavy skirt snagged on the log as she rolled in the current. Dan was by her side in an instant, untangling her and pulling her into his arms. Her face was deathly pale, her skin clammy, but he wrapped his arm under hers and stroked toward the shore.

His strength waning, Dan Gaines clenched his teeth and continued swimming across the slow heavy current his sodden boots tipping into a sand bar and he pushed himself to his feet. Lifting Rosa he staggered toward the rippling grass of the embankment collapsing in the damp grass and rolling Rosa to her side.

Hands shaking Dan bent her knees up trying to force the water she had swallowed out of her. "Please darlin' don't leave me," he moaned as he repeated the action. "Come back, I need you. Christina needs you. Rosa, Rosa," he sobbed as he pressed on her middle and water spilled from her mouth.

Rolling her on her side again Dan held her while she coughed, spewing the river water from her body like poison from a wound.

"You're gonna be all right," Dan crooned stroking her hair away from her face. "You're gonna be all right. I won't let anything happen to you." Tears stung his eyes as Rosa gasped for breath finally pulling in the fresh air as she sagged into him.

Dan pulled her close pressing her head to his chest. She was shaking, trembling now and his hot tears dropped onto her shoulder as they clung together. "I've got you, honey. I've got you." He dropped a gentle kiss to her head and sighed as she took another shuddering breath.

Dan clutched Rosa to him rocking her gently as he whispered silent thanks to God that she was alive. His heart was pounding and he was afraid he would never be able to release her.

"You came for me," Rosa whispered her voice

rough. "You risked everything."

"I'll always come for you Rosa," Dan said, all his feelings pouring from his soul. "I love you, and I'll do anything for you. I've never been so frightened in my life."

Rosa pushed herself away from him breaking his grip as she reared back to stare at him.

Dan's heart almost stopped as his hands shook with fear, hope, doubt, and relief. The emotions rolled over him faster and more chilling that the black waters of the big river. Without thinking he grasped Rosa's arms pulling her to him and dropping his lips to hers. Perhaps he would live to regret it, but in that instance, he had to hold her, taste her, and touch her.

Rosa's eyes went wide at Dan's words, and when he jerked her to him, she couldn't think. He couldn't love her. He didn't know her. As his lips met hers she blinked, everything whirling past like the muddy bottom of the river then she leaned into him grasping his dripping shirt in her hands as she kissed him back. As she surrendered to his kisses, his words echoed in her brain. He loved her.

Dan's chest burned as his breathing quickened and when Rosa wrapped her hands in his shirt, his heart began to race. She was here, in his arms kissing him back. He flinched as pain shot through his side and Rosa pulled away.

"I'm, I'm sorry," he said dropping his hands and looking away though he wasn't sorry at all. He knew Rosa would be angry. His lips burned longing to kiss her again as he waited for the inevitable tirade of words.

"You are hurt," Rosa gasped looking at the long cut along his ribs where bright red blood was oozing under his coat. "Let me look." Gently she pushed his coat back away from the cut, peeling the two sides of his slashed shirt aside.

"I guess that fella with the knife must have caught me. I don't remember."

"You could have been killed." Rosa reached down tearing a strip of cloth from her dripping petticoat as she pulled Dan's coat off and lifted his shirt.

Dan raised his arm as she peered at the wound. "It doesn't look too bad," he said offering her a slight grin. "I've had worse."

Rosa's dark eyes flashed at him as she began to wrap the cloth around his ribs stemming the flow of blood. "You will be lucky if you do not get infection." Rosa shivered at the thought and Dan pulled his coat around her. It was a good wool coat and would offer some warmth even wet.

"Come on," he said pushing himself to his feet and taking her cold hands. "We need to find shelter."

"Shouldn't we wait for the boat to return?" Rosa asked scanning the river for any sign of the vessel.

"Darlin' at this point I don't even know if they realize what happened. I think we're on our own."

Rosa shivered as the cool breeze gusted off of the river, and she struggled to rise, the weight of her sodden skirts making it difficult to stand.

Dan wrapped an arm around the little woman next to him steadying her as she struggled to her feet. She was shivering with cold, and he needed to find somewhere out of the wind for them so that they could warm up and dry out. He flinched as she clutched at him finding her balance, but he only tucked her closer trying to keep her warm.

Stepping out he helped Rosa through the long grass along the river, his eyes watching for any sign of danger. Neither of them spoke. There was too much to be said for mere words to suffice and only time would work out their fate. They had been walking for several minutes headed to the tree line when Dan stumbled and Rosa clutched at him lending her strength to his. Perhaps he had lost more blood than he realized when he was in the river. Either way, they were both exhausted and needed rest.

"Thank you," he whispered his arms tightening on Rosa as they stepped into a grove of trees that blocked the growing wind.

"Sit, you are too tired." Rosa insisted following him to a fallen log and helping him sit. "Perhaps there are houses nearby. I will go while you rest."

Dan's harsh chuckle made Rosa study him, her brows furrowing with an unspoken question.

"I don't think I'm letting you out of my sight," he laughed. "Besides you're already shivering with cold. We both need to get out of these wet clothes and get warmed up."

"How are we supposed to do that?" Rosa bridled placing her hand on her hips. "We are in the forest."

Dan patted the log next to him as exhaustion tugged at him. "Sit," he said, "I'll get a fire going and we'll strip down to our underthings so our clothes can dry."

"I will not," Rosa said her eyes flashing but her voice lacked the conviction it so often held.

"You will if you don't want to freeze to death," Dan laughed. "We're not in Needful anymore, and if I read the weather right, we're probably in for a storm. It's already cooling off not warming up, and the sun has been hidden most of the morning by clouds."

Rosa gazed around her and the signs forced her to agree. "I wish we could find someplace better," she mumbled, but another gust of wind rattled the treetops and she had to agree.

The wind picked up and the surrounding trees swayed making Rosa yelp. "What is that?" she asked as the grass flattened itself against the earth.

Dan turned, wincing at the pain in his side as he peered deeper into the grove. "Looks like a sod shack." He pushed himself to his feet and turned toward it bending to pick up a thick stick of wood on his way.

Rosa fell in behind him her wet clothing making her shiver again under the shadow of the trees. In a few minutes, they had reached the old cabin. It was covered in vines and the wood shake roof had moss growing on it, but it looked solid enough.

"I'll go in first," Dan whispered ducking low to step through the door. A flutter of wings and a family of doves startled him as they flew from the rafters and out a hole in the eaves. "It looks alright," he called to Rosa who stepped inside her stick raised in her hands.

"Check for snakes," Rosa breathed her eyes scanning the dust-covered floor. "There are always snakes."

Dan chuckled but made a careful turn around the small cabin. It had a wooden floor and stood a few feet off of the ground on thick logs. "No snakes," he grinned returning to the door. "The fireplace looks alright though and there's wood."

"What is this place do you think?" Rosa asked looking at the simple structure as she wrapped her arms around her middle trying to gain some warmth.

"Probably someone's fishing cabin, or maybe an old homesteader's place. At least it's shelter." He hurried to the fireplace looking into a box of kindling with a grin. "I'll get a fire started and hope the flue won't smoke us out."

Rosa wrapped her arms around herself as the wind whistled by. "You don't think anyone is coming for us?" she asked her dark eyes full of worry.

"We can't count on it," Dan said striking a piece of steel to a hard rock and urging the sparks to take. "There's no telling what is happening on the steamboat. With most of the passengers at breakfast, it might be dinner time until we're even missed."

The spark took and Dan added twigs and sticks to the flicker, blowing on it gently until a tongue of fire wrapped around a small branch. His teeth chattered as slowly he added wood to the fire watching that the smoke drifted upward, unobstructed by a nest of fallen leaves.

Rosa walked to the tiny fire sighing with relief as it caught and handing Dan a larger log. She was cold, wet, and exhausted. She wanted to be warm again, to feel the heat of Dan's kiss once more, and the assurance that she had survived.

"Now what do we do?" she asked as Dan rose.

"Now we get out of these wet things," Dan said walking to a box by the door and pulling out two old wool blankets. "I'm afraid it's the best we're going to get." He grinned. "This must be a fishing cabin or it wouldn't have anything inside."

Rosa nodded but didn't say anything as she turned her back on the man who had saved her life, slowly unbuttoning her dripping dress. If they stayed in their wet things for much longer, they would probably both die of cold.

As the gown slipped from her shoulders, she shivered then started as a warm blanket wrapped around her. It smelled of dust, and wood smoke, and she knew that Dan had been holding it by the fire to warm it. "Thank you," she whispered her heart swelling toward him as his word echoed once more in her brain. He had said he loved her. Could she believe him? Pulling the blanket tight and stepping out of her dress she realized that she desperately wanted to. She did not want to spend the rest of her life alone. What would it be like to truly be the wife of Dan Gaines, a wealthy rancher and Mayor of Needful?

Dan picked up Rosa's dress, the weight of it tugging at his wound and he hissed with pain.

"Your wound," Rosa said twisting to face him. She was wrapped in the thin blanket but her bare shoulders were still visible and Dan swallowed hard as his eyes traced the delicate line of her collar bone. He knew she was standing there in nothing but her shift and pantaloons and his blood heated at the thought. Turning on his heel he hurried back to the fire and hung her dress on a peg in the wall.

"You must change too," Rosa insisted. "Then I will check your wound."

The wind picked up outside and the first heavy drops of rain began to fall. Dan nodded, not daring to turn back to look at her as he began to unbutton his ruined shirt. In only moments he had stripped down to his draws under the scratchy blanket but he was still wet and cold. Holding the blanket with one hand he lifted another log into the fire and settled onto the dusty floor. "Come get warm," he called never turning his head. "No point freezing."

Rosa shuffled to where Dan sat before the fire holding her own blanket tight as she settled on the floor. They had shelter, warmth, and something to wrap themselves in. She had to thank God for that. Now if He would only help her figure out the feelings raging through her mind. She shivered and Dan snaked out an arm pulling her into his warmth and Rosa accepted it leaning her head on his shoulder as exhaustion, worry, and fear drained her of all energy.

"We'll be all right," Dan whispered his strong

arm holding her tight. "We just need to get warm and dry."

Rosa nodded against his shoulder letting the comfort of his strength roll over her. She didn't understand it, but she believed him and as her eyes drifted closed. She believed in his words as well. In her heart, Rosa knew that when he had said he loved her it was true.

Dan felt Rosa sag against his side as the rain drummed against the little cabin. He pulled her closer, wrapping the blanket a little tighter around her shoulders. She whimpered in her sleep and his grip tightened once more as their body heat began to meld.

The Mayor of Needful grinned as he leaned his head against Rosa's wondering how he'd ended up here. He should have been content now that he was completely alone with Rosa. He had her in his arms and wanted to keep her there, but how could he do it?

Chapter 24

A peel of thunder rolled over the cabin and Dan blinked awake. He was sprawled out on his back with something warm and soft practically on top of him. The orange glow of the dying fire lit the dim room and though he realized it must be midday, almost no sunlight reached them.

Tipping his chin downward he noticed Rosa splayed across him, her head resting on his chest as she slept. Somewhere along the way he must have nodded off to sleep and pulled Rosa with him onto the floor. He didn't mind though as he studied her bare arm draped across his chest. Rosa shifted snuggling closer and her hair fell into his face tickling his nose. Dan held in his chuckle trying to blow the offending strand away before it drove him crazy. Careful not to disturb her he grabbed the edge of the blanket that had fallen to the floor, flicking it over them and closed his eyes. He needed to build up the fire before the cabin grew cold and damp but he couldn't bring himself to disturb Rosa.

Again she wiggled closer, pressing tight against

his warmth, but when a shapely leg fell over his legs he groaned. "Rosa," he whispered. "Rosa, I need to build the fire up."

Rosa mumbled something then rolled over turning her back to him and suddenly grew still.

"Mayor Dan?" she queried her spine rigid.

"I'm here."

Rosa let out a breath pushing herself upright and blinking at the man. He lay on his back one arm pillowed beneath his head. "What are we doing on the floor?" She pushed herself into a sitting position trying to focus on her surroundings.

"I think we were sleeping," Dan's tone was light, teasing.

Rosa's cheeks flamed as she realized she had let the blanket slip and was sitting in her shift and bloomers next to Dan Gaines. She swallowed noticing the hungry, appraising look in his eyes and was shocked when he didn't look away.

"I thought you were going to build up the fire," she said tugging at the blanket that was stuck under his hip.

Dan chuckled pushing himself up on his elbows and watching Rosa squirm. Her hair had mostly fallen loose from its pins and fell around her in a tangled weave. Her eyes, dark and bright glimmered in the firelight. His eyes fell to her lips, and he licked his, his mouth suddenly going dry. Pushing himself upright he reached out brushing a lock of hair behind her ear and wondering if that was the one that had tickled his nose a moment ago.

"You look lovely," he drawled, his mind seemed to have slowed down and it could control the words his heart wished to speak.

Rosa dropped her eyes pulling her meager corner of the blanket to her breast but only drawing his eye there. Closing his eyes Dan willed himself not to reach for her. His arms trembled with the need, but instead, he rolled to his side and began placing logs on the fire coaxing it back to a bright and steady flame.

"How is your side?" Rosa asked her words punctuated by another crash of thunder.

Dan turned back, to reveal a broad chest smooth and well-muscled as well as the tight bandage around his ribs. "See for yourself," he offered, twisting to give her a better view.

Rosa reached out carefully her eyes tracing every line of his body. Her hands shook as she placed them along his ribs feeling for any heat or signs of swelling. "I think you will live," she spoke her hands still resting on his rib cage.

Dan dropped his hands to hers pressing them against his chest as he sat straighter. First lifting one and then the other he kissed each palm his eyes never leaving hers. A day ago, he had married her to save her from her father, now who would save her from him. His eyes burned with the knowledge that he loved her, but could never have her. He knew that she did not believe him to be an honorable man.

Rosa tugged, pulling her hand from his, but instead of rising and running away, she placed her palm on his cheek studying his face. His eyes never wavered from hers, though she knelt before him in next to nothing. His face was warm and the rough stubble of growth on his cheeks prickled against her palm.

"You meant what you said earlier?" Her voice sounded like a ragged croak and his lips twitched.

Placing his hand over hers he nodded, turning his head and kissing her palm once more. Heat that had nothing to do with the roaring fire, shot through her, and Rosa realized that she had a choice. She could pull away and lose this man's love, or she could let go and embrace it. For three long heartbeats, she studied his face searching for the truth that glowed in his blue eyes.

"Tell me again."

Dan sat up straighter, his face inches from hers as he met her dark eyes. "Rosa, I love you," he drawled. "At first I just wanted to look out for you for Raul, but..." he dropped his gaze his body sagging. "Somehow, I didn't mean to, but I fell in love with you."

Rosa pressed her hands to either side of her

new husband's face and smiled. "I did not know," she said. "I misjudged you, but..." she swallowed. "I see how you feel about me, and it does strange things to my heart. It gives me hope."

Dan pulled her close placing her on his outstretched legs and dropped his forehead to hers as his hands cupped her face. "All I want is a chance," he whispered. "A chance to show you that I love you and that I want to care for you and Christina. I don't expect you to love me. I just want a chance."

Rosa's soft intake of breath made Dan drop his hands, his eyes closing in pain as he understood her response. She couldn't do it. She was determined to make it on her own.

Rosa stared at the dejected features of the man she had wed and a single tear trickled from her eye as the shell around her heart cracked. How could he be willing to love her knowing she might never love him back? His simple words seemed to melt into her heart filling it with a flicker of hope and love. Letting go of the past she wrapped her arms around Dan's neck finding his lips in love's first kiss.

***

Dan woke for the second time that day to the soft patter of rain on the roof but this time everything came rushing back in a wave of heat and joy. Rosa was his. She had chosen him, and they lay together in a tangle of old blankets and half-dry clothes.

Rosa stirred in his arms, her eyes fluttering open as a shy smile broke across her face. "Hello."

"Hello," Dan grinned. He was half afraid to speak for fear that he would shatter the peace of the moment. He didn't know how to move forward with his little wife. He loved her, respected her, cared for her, but wasn't sure what to do.

"Is it still raining?" Rosa pulled the blankets around her as she sat up rubbing the sleep from her eyes.

"I think so," Dan offered sitting up and reaching for another log for the fire.

"Will you hang this up for me?" Rosa lifted the last of her garments toward him. "See if my dress is dry. We will need to find food soon."

Dan took the clothing from Rosa's hand leaning over impulsively to kiss the top of her head. Wrapping the second blanket around his waist, he hung the damp garments and checked her dress. "It's dry," he said lifting it from the hook and handing it to her.

"Turn around," Rosa insisted making him chuckle as he turned back to the fire and began stirring the embers with a stick.

Dan felt elated but cautious with the new relationship. As much as his heart had longed for Rosa, he wasn't sure what came next.

"You can turn around now," Rosa said. "I will go outside and you can dress." She gave him an appraising look that didn't match the modesty she had demanded a moment ago, but he nodded waiting until she stepped out into the door.

Quickly Dan pulled his scattered clothing back together slipping his hand through the slice in his best shirt with the shake of his head. His fingers lingered on the bandage wound around his ribs, but other than a twinge of pain, it felt fine.

The door swung open and he quickly buttoned his pants and shrugged into the shirt. His coat was still damp so he left it where it hung. Turning he smiled as Rosa looked up with him. She looked relaxed; her dark eyes shining then started to laugh as he scratched the back of his neck.

"It is dark outside." She said, tipping her head. "Why are you nervous?" Rosa moved to stand before him resting her hands on his sides as she looked up into his eyes. "You are worried that I will change my mind?"

"I don't know." Dan's hand stilled on the back of his neck. "I don't know what to expect next."

Rosa's bright smile lit up his heart and he started to relax. "Daniel Gaines, I am not a fickle woman. Hot-tempered yes," Rosa laughed. "I did not know how you felt, and I am sorry that I thought bad things about you."

"It's alright," Dan jumped in. "Now that I know, I understand and I don't blame you."

Rosa released him pacing the room in a few quick steps. "After Raul and what he did, I thought that there would be no love for me again. I could not hope that it was possible. Not for who I am, what I am. Raul knew who I was and chose me, anyway. When I found out what he did. How he borrowed money from his outlaw brother, it made me angry. I felt betrayed by the man I loved and lost. I did not hope for anything more. I have Christina and that is enough." The petite woman turned, pacing the room again as she wrapped her arms around her middle. "I do not know why you love me," she stopped her back to him, "but I will accept it. I must learn to trust again."

In two long strides, Dan was behind her pulling her into his arms and pressing her close to his heart. "I didn't expect any of this." His voice caught in his throat, but he forced himself to continue. "When I made you that offer right after Raul was killed, I meant it for what it was: a way to provide for the wife and daughter of my friend. I was eaten up with guilt that I hadn't been able to save him. If I had known I would have given him the money to pay Rivera back. Later I was eaten up with guilt for the way I felt about you."

Rosa closed her eyes the pain of losing Raul springing fresh in her heart once more, as she sought comfort in Dan's arms.

"Later," Dan rested his chin against her head letting his words fall around them. "Later, I grew to respect you for who you were even if every time I tried to talk to you we fought."

Rosa's chuckle rippled through his chest and Dan grinned. "You are a very stubborn woman you know." He pulled back looking down into her face. "I didn't even know I was falling in love with you until your father came to town. When he threatened to take you from Needful, I thought my world would end. I couldn't let you go."

"That is why you did what you did?" Rosa said looking into his blue eyes amazed at his confession.

Dan nodded. "Then I felt guilty for wanting you. You were Raul's wife, and he was my friend. I thought it was wrong, but I still couldn't let you go. Even if only to keep you from having to return to Mexico with your father or to give you a chance to live the life you chose for yourself, I was willing to do this."

"I'm glad you did," Rosa admitted. "I was so wrapped up in my pain and sorrow that I could not believe you had good intentions. I did not want to be dependent on a man again. As much as I loved Raul, and as much as I understand why he did what he did, I was hurt and angry. Trusting after such pain is difficult."

Dan placed his finger under her chin and lifted her eyes to his once more. "Are you ready to try now?"

Rosa nodded. "I would not have kissed you, been with you, if I was not." Her face heated but Dan's lips found hers once more chasing away the embarrassment and reminding her that she was a woman, newlywed.

Chapter 25

Dan pulled back from the kiss his heart racing and smiled down at Rosa. He would end up with a crook in his neck at this rate.

"Now what?" he asked, knowing instinctively he should give Rosa the lead.

"Now you go catch us some dinner." Rosa's bright laugh filled the room and Dan threw back his head joining her as joy filled them both with new hope.

"All right," he chuckled kissing her once more before heading for the door. "I'll see if I can snare a rabbit or something."

He was only able to find a few wild potatoes for them to roast in the fire but that night he started a whole new life with the woman he loved.

***

Dan eased his way through the small clump of trees that protected them from much of the weather. A cool drizzle of rain misted through the leaves as his eyes scanned the ground looking for any sign of rabbits or other wild game. He had set up a snare the night before and hoped they'd have some luck this morning. As soon as the weather broke he and Rosa would have to start looking for a town.

The sound of voices near the river caught his attention and his head snapped up as he hurried back the way he had just come.

Slipping behind a tree, he gazed out across the grassland he and Rosa had climbed out on expecting to see a boat on the river, he wasn't prepared to see his brother easing a horse through the rushes scanning for sign.

"Spencer!" Dan shouted rushing out of the trees and waving his brother down as other riders moved toward him.

"I thought my days of dragging you out of trouble were over long ago," Spencer shouted back with a grin. "Don't you know you're supposed to be on your honeymoon, not camping out in the woods?" he scanned the area pushing his horse into a trot until he stopped before his brother. "Where's Rosa?" Spencer's voice was tight with fear.

"She's fine," Dan breathed reaching out and clasping his brother's hand. "We found a little cabin in the woods."

Spencer visibly relaxed as Juan Xavier and a few of his men joined them.

"Rosa's fine." The brothers called out together, laughing and breaking the dark tension that swirled around the other man.

"How d'you get here so fast?" Dan asked looking back toward the cabin before confronting the other men. "We only went overboard yesterday morning."

"A rider brought us a wire," Spencer said. "Which reminds me, as you are the mayor, I think you should think about getting a telegraph to Needful. Anyway, this rider came in. The wire said you'd been thrown overboard by two men who had been robbing the guests on the riverboat. Some man named Harold had found them knocked out on the deck with his wife's jewelry in their pockets. When they came to, he got the story out of them."

Dan sighed with relief. "I wouldn't have expected that," he admitted. "I'm just glad to see you."

"Where is my daughter?" Juan Xavier asked. "I would like to see her."

"Better bring food then," Dan chuckled waiting as both men dismounted and followed him into the trees. A moment later his knuckles fell on the damp door of the little cabin and Rosa opened it.

"Father!" Rosa gasped as Dan stepped through the door leading their guests.

Juan Xavier pulled Rosa into a deep hug. "I am so sorry," he said. "If I had thought you were in danger, I never would have insisted."

Rosa pulled out of his arms, her hand sliding into Dan's. "I am fine," she said. "I have a man who cares about me enough to risk his neck to save me." She smiled up at Dan, and for the first time, he knew that everything would be all right.

"Can we go home now?" Rosa looked between Dan and Spencer, her eyes pleading. "I want to see my daughter. We have much to do as we start this new life."

Dan nodded squeezing her hand. "How about lunch?" he teased.

"We won't get home before dark if we leave now," Spencer reminded her. "Why don't we set up camp outside, and we'll head for Needful first thing in the morning. It's a long ride."

Rosa nodded accepting the sense of it, though her heart longed for home. A new home. A new start in Needful.

Soon the little cabin was full of the men from the search party, and she was cooking what they had brought with them over the fire while Spencer explained that under questioning the men who had thrown her overboard had given a rough idea of where they had gone into the water.

"We switched horses three times to get here as

soon as we did," he grinned. "Juan Xavier wouldn't slow down if it meant he had to buy all the horses himself."

Rosa turned to her father. "Thank you," she said, truly meaning it. Perhaps, in time, she would be able to forgive her father for his selfishness all those years before. For now, she was just thankful that he had come for her, and that she would be home soon.

The next evening, an exhausted Rosa slid from the saddle she had shared with Dan through the long ride home and into the arms of Olive Hampton.

"Oh my goodness," the older woman glared up at the mayor. "Only gone a day, and he almost loses you." Olive pulled Rosa along with her into the Hampton House ignoring Dan as he dismounted, hitching his weary mount to the hitching rail.

"Looks like I'm in trouble again," he grumbled, shooting a hard look at his brother. He had no sooner ridden into town than his wife was whisked away from him, and he was wondering if they would ever have a moment alone again. Trudging into the Hampton House, Dan stepped into the bustle of the dining hall; the smells of savory food making his stomach turn over with hunger.

"Dan!" Daliah cheered hurrying to him and hugging him tightly. "I'm glad you're back and all right," she added looking between him and Rosa who was covering her daughter's face with kisses.

"It's good to be home," Dan grinned. "I think a lot has changed in a very short time," he added.

Rosa looked up smiling across the room at him and Daliah grinned seeing what he meant. "I think so," she said squeezing his arm lightly then turning to step outside to greet her husband.

"Daliah," Rosa called before the woman was through the door. "I will bring Daniel to you soon. He has a wound I would like you to see to."

Daliah raised her brows, her dark eyes turning to Dan accusingly.

"I'm fine," Dan said his voice tired.

Daliah nodded once then left him to face the Hamptons on his own.

A moment later he, Rosa, Christina, Olive, and Orville were seated at a table as hot meals were served and they recounted the tale of their adventure. It seemed like a lifetime ago that he had leapt over the railing of the boat, plunging into the dark waters below without a thought for himself.

"Well it's about time," Olive said looking between Dan and Rosa. "I thought you two hated each other."

Rosa laughed leaning into Dan as Christina giggled with delight.

"Pay up boys," Orville called to his three sons who had gathered around the table to hear the tale. "I told you I was right, and your ma was wrong on this one."

Olive looked at Orville shock on her face. "What was I wrong about?"

"You was convinced you needed to find a wife for our Dan here," the old man laughed. "I was pretty sure she was already in town."

Olive looked between her husband and the couple on the other side of the table from her and shook her head. All these months she had been sending for mail-order brides hoping the right one would come along for the Mayor of Needful, and all the while, she was living under her own roof. "I thought this was just a fake wedding," she whispered to Rosa.

"I thought so too," Rosa admitted with a shrug. "Somehow, it became real."

Dan stroked his thumb along Rosa's jaw, his blue eyes full of love as he pecked her on the cheek. "Can we go home now?" he asked.

"No, no you can't" Olive sprang to her feet as her hands landed on her hips. "You just got back and you can stay right here for the night. Then we'll get you and Rosa moved tomorrow." A hint of sorrow tinged her voice as she looked at Rosa, but it was quickly chased away by her smile. "It sure isn't what I expected," she said shaking her head, "but I'm happy for the both of you."

Laughter filled the room as the family let the relief of one of their own returning home sweep over them.

Sometimes life didn't go the way you planned, but it had a way of working itself out in the long run. Through joy and sorrow, cheer, and pain, life moved forward carrying you along like the flow of a mighty river and as long as your bark was held by the Almighty's hand, you could be sure to see your way safely to the sea when the time came.

Epilogue

Rosa bustled into the kitchen of the sprawling ranch house. This house was very different than the two-story home of her friend Primrose, but she had fallen in love with it. There was a large kitchen, a comfortable, if masculine, living area, and four bedrooms. Tying an apron around her waist she settled Christina into her high chair and stoked the fire to life.

A smile flickered across her face as she heard footsteps down the hall and knew that Dan would be there soon. It hadn't taken long for the Hamptons to move her meager belongings into Dan's already established house. For the first time in nearly two years, Rosa felt content. She was loved, valued, and wanted.

Dan crept up behind her, leaning down and wrapping his arms around her middle. "Good morning little wife," he said kissing the back of her neck then laughing as little Christina squealed.

Rosa lifted strips of bacon into a heavy frying pan as she tried to shrug her husband off. "I am trying to cook," she grumbled hiding her smile by studying the stove. "You will go hungry if you keep doing that."

Dan laughed kissing her neck again and nuzzling her cheek. "Sooner or later you'll feed me."

Rosa laughed as he backed away and lifted two cups from a shelf. "I'll get the coffee going?"

"I think Cookie already started it," Rosa said indicating the pot simmering on the back burner. "He is sneaky that one."

Dan shook his head testing the pot and pouring the dark brew into the tin cups. He had been afraid that Rosa and Cookie were going to kill each other when he had first brought his new family home, but now they seemed to dance around each other keeping a balance in the kitchen and the men fed at the same time.

Placing the cups on the table he lifted Christina from her chair kissing her. "How's my best girl," he crooned tickling the little girl with his stubbly cheek.

"I thought I was your best girl," Rosa said turning and shaking a fork at him as her eyes glowed with delight at how he was with her daughter.

"Who says I can't have two best girls?" Dan said reaching out and grabbing her wrist as he pulled her to him in a quick twirl. "See two arms, one for each of you," he laughed dipping his head and kissing Rosa again.

"I'll burn the bacon if you don't let me go," Rosa said soaking in the warmth of his kiss.

"We wouldn't want that," Dan gasped releasing her. "If you burn the bacon Cookie will insist on taking over the cooking again."

Rosa bristled making Dan laugh harder as she returned to her work. Rosa loved cooking and he loved teasing her about letting Cookie take over. The smell of bacon filled the room, joined a moment later by the sizzle of eggs hitting the hot pan. His stomach rumbled, but his heart soared. His whole world had been turned upside down by the beautiful woman cooking his breakfast.

Dan could barely remember what it was like before Rosa and Christina had become his family. He had never thought his life before his wedding was empty, but now he couldn't imagine how lost he would be without his two best girls.

Rosa plated bacon and eggs placing it on the table before him and grabbing one for her and Christina as well. She loved the morning routine and the quiet time with her family before the day began.

Soon she would be helping Cookie prepare breakfast for the rest of the hands. On days when she missed the Hamptons or wanted to go to town the old camp cook was more than able to manage, and it made it even more fun when she insisted that he had done it all wrong. In truth, Rosa adored the old man and the freedom he afforded her as the wife of the rancher and Mayor of Needful

Dan reached out taking her hand in one of his and touching Christina's with the other as he bowed his head.

"Dear Lord," his voice carried strong and confident through the kitchen. "Thank you for this new day and a chance to do the work you've set before us. Thank you for this food and the bounty of your provision. And thank you for the love you've given me in this family I never expected to have. I am humbled by the gifts you have given and will try to always remember to be thankful." He looked up catching Rosa's dark eyes studying him and smiled. "Amen," he finished but didn't let go of her hand.

"I am very thankful for you as well," Rosa said a bright tear trickling down her cheek. "I did not know that I could find happiness again."

Dan lifted her hand kissing it softly as his heart filled with love, joy, and hope. "I love you darlin'," he said. "I don't know what I ever did to deserve this life, but I'm mighty thankful for it."

"I love you too," Rosa said her smile mingled with joy, hope, and sorrow melting his heart. She had seen many sorrows in her life, but if you were willing to take the chance, a new start could be right before your eyes if you could be brave enough to look.

"Are you two done making googley-eyes at each other or should I go back outside," Cookie said stomping into the kitchen and casting a critical eye over the stove.

Dan leaned over kissing Rosa with a big smacking kiss and making the old man groan.

"It ain't decent two folks being so happy," the old man said slicing bacon and starting on the bigger breakfast for the ranch hands. "I think I liked you better when you was just pining for the girl. You were more interesting."

"Cookie!" Christina gurgled banging a spoon on the top of her highchair tray. "Cookie!"

The old man turned, his gappy smile widening as his eyes filled with love. "No, you're a sensible one," he growled reaching into the warming tray and taking down a sugar cookie before handing it to the little girl.

"Why you sneak," Rosa said releasing Dan's hand and moving to the stove. "No wonder she calls you every time you step into the kitchen."

The old man slapped his knee laughing as Rosa glared at him.

Dan grinned finishing his breakfast with a full heart. Home was so much more than the word had ever meant before, and he couldn't wait to see what came next.

The End

More Brides of Needful Texas

Daliah

Prim

Peri

Beth

Ruth

Sign up for my Newsletter and get a free book! Subscribe **or follow on** Bookbub at Facebook & AllAuthor

Other Books by this Author:
From the Cattleman's Daughters

Katie	Isabella
Fiona	Alexis
Meg	Mae

Cattleman's Daughters Companions

Cathleen

The Redemption of Rachel

Sean's Secret Heart

Mel

Sweet Annie

Joan

Tales from Biders Clump

Christmas Kringle

Quil's Careful Cowboy

Bruno's Belligerent Beauty

Tywyn'sTroubles

A Teaching Touch

Prissy's Predicament

Lucinda's Luck

Ferd's Fair Favor

The Travels of Titus

Winter's Worth

Strong Hearts: Open Spirits

Maggie's Valley   Sadina's Stocking

Celestre's Song   Beloved Beulah

Whispers in Wyoming

Love Letters & Home

Counting Kadence

Mercy's Light

Falling Forward

Racing Destiny

Baby be Mine

The Ornamental Match Maker

Carousel Horse Christmas

Loose Goose Christmas

Pineapple Persuasion

July's Jubilant Christmas Jumble

Shutter Shock Christmas in July

If you enjoyed this book check out more books by Danni Roan at Amazon Or follow me on Facebook, Twitter, Bookbub & AllAuthor

If you'd like to get updates on my work, see special sneak peeks and be entered in special contests sign up for my newsletter on my webpage or my amazon author page

For more amazing Western Historical Romance join me and my friends at Pioneer Hearts a Facebook group for readers like you.

Dear Reader,

Thank you for choosing to read my book. I hope you have enjoyed it as much as I've enjoyed writing it. If you enjoyed the story, please feel free to leave a review wherever you purchased the book. Leaving a review will help me and prospective readers to know what you liked about this book. It is an opportunity for your voice to be heard and for you to tell others why the story is worth a read.

About the Author

Danni Roan, a native of western Pennsylvania, spent her childhood roaming the lush green mountains on horseback. She has always loved westerns and specifically western romance and is thrilled to be part of this exciting genre. She has lived and worked overseas with her husband and tries to incorporate the unique quality of the people she has met throughout the years into her books.

Danni currently lives in her thirty-six foot RV with her husband and is traveling the United States to see this beautiful country and experience its history first hand.

Danni and her 'every-day-hero' have one son who is attending college and finding his own way as his crazy parents experience the author life along with life on the road.

As a Christian Danni, believes strongly that God brings new challenges, and blessings into one's life to help them grow and she hopes that her words were both and encouragement and inspiration to you.

Made in the USA
Columbia, SC
26 March 2022

58183409R00124